PRAISE FOR
THE BACKSTAGERS
SERIES

"Applauseworthy."
—*Kirkus Reviews*

"[Mientus] preserves
the spirit and flavor of the
comics with hilarious pranks and
theater talk, high-energy hustle, and,
particularly, in a young cast, notably diverse
in ethnic and gender identity, who face personal
issues common to everyone."
—*Booklist*

THE BACKSTAGERS

AND THE
FINAL BLACKOUT

BOOK THREE

BY **ANDY MIENTUS**
ILLUSTRATED BY **RIAN SYGH**

BASED ON THE BACKSTAGERS COMICS
CREATED BY JAMES TYNION IV & RIAN SYGH

AMULET BOOKS

NEW YORK

PUBLISHER'S NOTE: THIS IS A WORK OF FICTION. NAMES, CHARACTERS, PLACES, AND INCIDENTS ARE EITHER THE PRODUCT OF THE AUTHOR'S IMAGINATION OR USED FICTITIOUSLY, AND ANY RESEMBLANCE TO ACTUAL PERSONS, LIVING OR DEAD, BUSINESS ESTABLISHMENTS, EVENTS, OR LOCALES IS ENTIRELY COINCIDENTAL.

THE LIBRARY OF CONGRESS HAS CATALOGED THE HARDCOVER EDITION AS FOLLOWS:

NAMES: MIENTUS, ANDY, AUTHOR. | SYGH, RIAN, ILLUSTRATOR.

TITLE: THE BACKSTAGERS AND THE FINAL BLACKOUT / BY ANDY MIENTUS ; ILLUSTRATED BY RIAN SYGH.

DESCRIPTION: NEW YORK, NY : AMULET BOOKS, 2019. | SERIES: THE BACKSTAGERS ; [3] | SUMMARY: A MYSTERIOUS MASKED MAN HAS STOLEN ALL OF THE ARTIFACTS AND IT IS UP TO THE BACKSTAGERS, EACH WITH HIS OR HER OWN UNIQUE SKILLS, TO RETRIEVE THEM.

IDENTIFIERS: LCCN 2019018609 | ISBN 9781419738654 (HARDBACK)

SUBJECTS: CYAC: THEATER—FICTION. | CLUBS—FICTION. | MAGIC—FICTION. | SUPERNATURAL—FICTION. | HIGH SCHOOLS—FICTION. | SCHOOLS—FICTION. | BISAC: JUVENILE FICTION / PERFORMING ARTS / THEATER. | JUVENILE FICTION / ACTION & ADVENTURE / GENERAL. | JUVENILE FICTION / SOCIAL ISSUES / FRIENDSHIP.

BISAC: JUVENILE FICTION / PERFORMING ARTS / THEATER. | JUVENILE FICTION / ACTION & ADVENTURE / GENERAL. | JUVENILE FICTION / SOCIAL ISSUES / FRIENDSHIP.

CLASSIFICATION: LCC PZ7.1.M519 BAB 2019 | DDC [FIC]—DC23

LC RECORD AVAILABLE AT HTTPS://LCCN.LOC.GOV/2019018609

PAPERBACK ISBN 978-1-4197-4354-2

TEXT AND ILLUSTRATIONS COPYRIGHT © 2019 BOOM! STUDIOS

BOOK DESIGN BY CHAD W. BECKERMAN

THE BACKSTAGERS CREATED BY RIAN SYGH & JAMES TYNION IV.

THE BACKSTAGERS ™ AND © RIAN SYGH & JAMES TYNION IV.

PRINTED AND BOUND IN U.S.A.

10 9 8 7 6 5 4 3 2 1

AMULET BOOKS ARE AVAILABLE AT SPECIAL DISCOUNTS WHEN PURCHASED IN QUANTITY FOR PREMIUMS AND PROMOTIONS AS WELL AS FUNDRAISING OR EDUCATIONAL USE. SPECIAL EDITIONS CAN ALSO BE CREATED TO SPECIFICATION. FOR DETAILS, CONTACT SPECIALSALES@ABRAMSBOOKS.COM OR THE ADDRESS BELOW.

AMULET BOOKS® IS A REGISTERED TRADEMARK OF HARRY N. ABRAMS, INC.

ABRAMS The Art of Books
195 Broadway, New York, NY 10007
abramsbooks.com

FOR THE COMMUNITY THAT KEEPS ME LOVING THEATER, EVEN WHEN IT DOESN'T FEEL LIKE IT LOVES ME BACK. YOU KNOW WHO YOU ARE.

PROLOGUE

WHEN YOU GO TO THE BOOKSTORE OR THE LIBRARY, FIND THE DRAMA section (if they still have one anymore), and pull a title off the shelf, you may think you're holding a play. That's understandable. The title on the front cover is the same title as a famous play. The playwright listed below is also the writer of that famous play. It may even have pictures from one of the play's productions on the cover or printed inside. It contains all of the dialogue, characters, and action of the play. But still, it isn't a play.

Nonsense, you say, but think about it: The bound paper you hold in your hands is merely instructions on how to perform the play, like a recipe or a user manual. Or maybe a book of spells is more like it. For, much like a book of spells, the words certainly contain magic, but not as they lay there, lifeless, on the printed page. For the magic to take place, you must assemble the necessary materials, prepare the space, dim the lights, and speak those words aloud with great feeling and intention. Only then do you really have a play, and only then do you begin to access the real magic that lies hidden deep within the ancient art we call theater. It is as old as anything we know in this world and is discovered and rediscovered, again and again, by each new generation as they pick up one of those books of spells, take it to a bare stage, and begin to manifest the play into reality.

There was a time though, very very long ago, when that magic wasn't hidden behind velvet curtains and masks of tragedy, when it was newly dreamed up, as most magical things are, by a young and curious mind.

The boy's breath burned in his chest as he ran across the grassy lawn, away from the jagged black cliff, toward the white clay house where his mother was hanging linen out to dry in the perfect spring sunshine.

He shouted, "Mother, mother! Come quickly! I have to show you!"

The boy's mother looked up from her work, smiling at her son, so easily delighted. What would it be this time?

A particularly colorful beetle? Maybe a bird's nest hanging in an olive tree? Her smile faded ever so slightly when she noticed for the first time how quickly he was growing. But she was warmed by the knowledge that as long as he still came bounding up to her, eyes glinting with excitement to share some beautiful thing with her, he'd still be her little boy.

"My darling, can it wait? I'm almost finished with the washing."

"I worked so hard! And I'm finally done!" He wasn't so much whining as he was singing with excitement.

"Well, if *your* work is done, then, my goodness, I'm sure mine can wait," she said, chuckling.

The boy beamed just the way the sun rose over the sea below their little cliffside home. He took his mother's hand and practically swept her off her feet as he charged back toward the cliff.

"Careful, my son, the rocks! You don't want to send us both tumbling down toward Poseidon!" She laughed, though the cliff did hang a serious distance above the churning, frothy sea.

"I'm not afraid of that old barnacle," the boy roared into the salty air. "He's going to be afraid of me, now!"

"Let's not boast, dear," she said, before mouthing a silent apology toward the dark water on the horizon.

The boy led his mother, not as carefully as she'd like, down some stairs that wrapped along the side of the cliff, and soon they reached a landing. Mercifully, the mother thought.

Where the flat landing met the steep side of the cliff, there was a shallow rectangular outcropping that housed the mouth of a cave. The mother didn't love that her son had chosen this precarious spot as his secret hideout, but then, she was looking to hide him from the world as long as she could and a cave like this seemed as good a hiding spot as any.

"Wait HERE!" he commanded, darting into the cave, leaving her a blessed moment of quiet to catch her breath. *He will be very hard to keep up with in a few years*, she thought.

The boy emerged from the cave at a fraction of the speed with which he'd entered it, because now his arms were overflowing with strange objects. His mother's brow furrowed a bit as she watched him lay out each item before him with a care she had never seen from her usually careless or carefree son.

"I've been working on them for weeks," he said. "I didn't want to show you until they were finished. And now they are FINISHED!" He waved his hand toward the array, inviting her to take a look.

His mother didn't quite know what she was looking at, even though her eyes were pointing in the right direction. A rod of metal with a glass ball at the tip. A piece of oblong stone with some symbols carved into the sides. A brick of wood with a groove cut into its center. A leather belt. A wooden box. And two curious scrolls.

Her confused eyes met his expectant ones. She didn't know what to say.

"They're . . . they're beautiful! I love that you are being creative. Maybe you can bring some of that energy to the kitchen; I think it's time for lunch!"

She turned to head back up the steep stairs when the boy cried, "But you have to see what they DO!"

"Maybe after lunch, my dar—"

And suddenly the boy's mother couldn't speak, because the sun had fallen out of the sky and their perfect spring afternoon was now a moonless night.

She turned back to the boy, terrified. He held the wooden block, his finger at the very bottom of the groove cut down its center.

"Don't be scared!" he said. "We have this!"

He put down the wooden block and picked up the metal rod. As he held it aloft, the glass ball at its end illuminated brilliantly, casting a perfect sphere of white light around them.

"Nothing can hurt us while we're in here. Um, hold

it, please." He thrust the strange glowing object into his mother's trembling hand and picked up the oblong stone.

"Now, this one is—" He brought it up to his lips and touched one of the symbols carved upon it. **"ONE OF MY FAVORITES."** His voice bellowed, impossibly loud, throughout the countryside.

"Dionysus, that's ENOUGH!" his mother screamed, dropping the glowing rod as if it were flaming hot. The boy's eyes grew wide and he picked up the wooden block again. With a swipe of his finger, from the bottom of its groove to the middle, the sun returned to its rightful place in the sky. The birds began to chirp, and everything was right again. Except for his mother, who stood paralyzed with terror.

A gentle roll of thunder snapped her out of the stupor. She turned toward the sound and saw a small gathering of storm clouds a few miles out above the sea. They seemed to creep toward the cliffside, closer every moment.

The mother dropped to her knees to look her son in the eye and said, "Listen to me, Dionysus. You need to hide these things, now."

"But you haven't even seen what all of them can do!"

"And I don't want to! This power you have harnessed— it's far too much for someone your age. And a demigod, no less."

Dionysus didn't like that term one bit. He looked at her defiantly and said, "It's my power. I made these objects. Why can't I use them?"

"Because your father is very jealous!" she whispered, looking over her shoulder to the encroaching storm. "If he thinks a half-mortal son of his has surpassed his power, there's no telling what he might do."

Dionysus looked toward the dark clouds himself and nodded, his shoulders slumped.

"But," his mother offered, "I didn't say you can't use it, I said you must hide it. We just have to be very clever."

"What do you mean?" Dionysus asked.

"Well, we can keep these things deep in the cave there. No one ever goes inside except for you, right? Not even Zeus will know. We'll build a door to the cave and inside, you'll be safe to let your powers free."

"But then no one will see them but me," he said, dejected.

"And me, silly! Think of all the wonderful things you'll be able to show me, when you get really good with these powers. You can put on wonderful shows for me whenever you want."

He thought for a moment, then asked, "What if I can figure out a way to keep the magic hidden and still put on shows for everyone? So that they experience my magic but never know how I'm doing it?"

"That would be very powerful magic indeed," his mother said. "Now quick, get into the cave. There is a storm coming."

Together, they gathered up Dionysus's magical objects and took cover deep inside his secret cave as thunder boomed and clapped in the distance.

CHAPTER 1

B*OOM.*
CLAP.
Boom.
CLAP.

It was almost like magic the way some colored lights, hanging streamers, and thumping music could turn the St. Genesius auditorium from a banal, beige chamber of athletic horrors to a candy-colored wonderland. But it was more like a curse the way suits, dresses, and the expectation of dancing in front of their crushes could turn the generally confident students of St. Genesius and Penitent Angels into sweaty, insecure messes.

Beneath a huge banner reading SPRING DANCE AT THE GYM hundreds of teenagers attempted to move and shake themselves in a way that might be interpreted as human dancing. They looked as comfortable piloting their own bodies as they might be piloting alien spacecrafts. Luckily the lights were very low.

That was by the design of Beckett and Sasha, who surveyed the wiggling crowd from the safety of the refreshments table.

"Look at them," Beckett said to Sasha, as he ladled some punch into a red plastic cup. "Some of these budding romances might actually survive tonight, thanks to us!" His neon blue tux, neon green hair, and neon purple plugs flashed especially bright in the pulsating light. Being able to create an atmosphere specifically to enhance your look is an advantage the other guys at Genesius would have killed for in this moment.

"You think Coach Barry will pass us in gym now?" Sasha's already anime-sized eyes swelled to planetary proportions.

"That was the deal, my man. And we did good!" Beckett raised his hand for a high five and Sasha had to leap up to meet it, nearly tearing the seams of his tiny black tux.

"Where are the rest of the guys?" Sasha asked, readjusting his floppy blond curls.

"They're easy to spot," Beckett replied with a smirk. "Look for the only guys actually having a good time."

Sasha scanned the crowd and discovered that was very

true, for among the hoard of stiff and stammering students trying desperately to look cool, there was one group of kids, way off in the corner, who didn't care about looking cool at all.

Jory, feeling fresh with an immaculate fade and a burgundy suit he'd designed himself, strutted around the dance floor like a disco king while his boyfriend, Hunter, opting for comfort in a tux-print T-shirt and vintage black blazer, howled with laughter. Hunter erupted in applause when Jory ended his dance with a dramatic pose, pointing at Aziz, cueing him to take the space for a dance solo of his own.

Aziz was characteristically conservative in an all-black ensemble, but when it was time to get down, he was anything but buttoned-up as he nailed a perfect Running Man before dropping into a split (which absolutely no one knew he could do) and passing the floor to Reo.

Reo shut his eyes and let the music surge through his body as if it were possessing him before he started spinning around the floor, his dark velvet robes and skirt swirling around him like incense smoke. The group whooped and cheered until Reo turned on his heel and took a bow.

"I hope that was a spell to cleanse the space of awkward," Beckett hollered over the music as he and Sasha joined their friends.

"If only I were that powerful," Reo said. "Sasha, I give you the floor."

With a dramatic sweep of his hand, Reo welcomed Sasha into the center of the circle. Without missing a beat, Sasha hit the floor and began wiggling his little body like an electrified worm as his fellow Backstagers roared. The electric worm squirmed to a dramatic death before he pointed to Beckett, who rolled his eyes.

"Come on, Beck!" Sasha said. "You're not scared to look dumb, are you?"

"Of course not," Beckett said. "Why would I be—"

Suddenly Beckett's face turned a neon red to match his neon suit and hair, because he locked eyes with Bailey Brentwood, the Coolest Girl in the World (and his all-but-official girlfriend), as she approached arm in arm with her best friend, Adrienne. They were both stunning: Bailey in a yellow dress, short and lightweight for maximum dance-floor mobility, and Adrienne in a sparkly rose-gold romper that matched her rose-gold hair and rosy cheeks perfectly.

"Crap, I ruined it!" Bailey moaned. "I thought I was finally gonna see Beckett dance!"

"Yeah, close call," Beckett muttered as he looked to the floor.

Bailey snorted as she threw her arm around Beckett affectionately.

"You look amazing!" Aziz said to Adrienne. She smiled and pointed up toward the thumping speakers.

"*ASL, please!*" she signed. Aziz chuckled and put his face in his hands—duh! Normally Adrienne was comfortable lip-reading with her hearing aids in, but against the music, Aziz should have known signing would be better. Luckily, now that they were an official couple, Aziz was getting more fluent every day. He repeated himself in ASL and she blushed and took a turn, modeling her sparkles.

The rhythmic pop song gave way to something slow and romantic, and you could feel the temperature in the room rise as hundreds of teenagers all panicked in unison.

"I think it's time to make our escape," Aziz said and signed.

"*Why?*" Adrienne signed.

"*The music*," he replied. "*Slow. Sappy.*" He threw out every cheesy romantic sign he could remember, his face contorted in a silly pucker, and Adrienne laughed.

"Backstagers, that's our cue!" Hunter announced to the group. "To the Club Room!"

Very happily, the crew followed Hunter toward the exit of the gym. Bailey, however, grabbed Beckett's shoulder.

"Wait," she said. "Now, I know you're not the most . . . graceful, but I think you can handle a slow dance, right? I mean it's literally just swaying."

"In theory . . ." Beckett said, his palms sweating.

"Let me handle this," she said as she took his hand and began to sway to the beat. "You okay so far?"

"I am very, very okay," he said, as his blushing cheeks returned to their normal color and the tension in his shoulders began to relax. He'd wanted to be exactly in this moment ever since he'd met Bailey when he was a student at Penitent Angels, and now, miraculously, here they were.

Jory and Hunter were hand in hand and almost out the gym doors when they looked back and saw Beckett and Bailey beginning to sway to the music. Jory looked at Hunter like a proud parent and they left the dancing couple to their romantic moment.

After a few moments, Beckett allowed his body to give way to the music, and soon he and Bailey moved in sync beneath a glittering disco ball, which cast a galaxy of white lights around them.

"It's been such a crazy year, hasn't it?" Bailey asked.

"Bonkers," Beckett said.

Together, they'd conquered four musicals built from the ground up, school work, crises small and large in their friend groups, and (most impressively) their own nerves and anxiety as they finally opened up to each other about their romantic feelings. Then there was all the world-saving that had kept Beckett busy as he escaped a magical limbo, battled an ultra-powerful ghost, and foiled the evil plans of a nefarious organization, all unbeknownst to Bailey.

"But I'm feeling pretty great about where things have ended up," Bailey said, dropping her eyes.

"Yeah," Beckett said with a nervous chuckle. "It feels most definitely worth it."

Bailey looked up again into Beckett's eyes, but her expression had changed ever so subtly. Her usual Bailey Brentwood twinkle had been replaced with something deeper and more serious. Beckett realized that it was his first time ever seeing her nervous. She shut her eyes and leaned toward him. It took Beckett a moment to even realize that he was about to have his first kiss.

Beckett's mind was usually so crowded with thoughts about electrical grids, sound mixing, and Diet Coke that he had never really imagined what his first kiss might be like, let alone a kiss with someone he cared for as much as Bailey. He had seen some miraculous things in the backstage— flowing rivers of rainbow paint, swarms of winged stage lights blinking every imaginable color, lavish ballrooms full of gowns that danced on their own—but this moment was the greatest bit of magic he'd ever experienced. He shut his eyes and tried to imprint it on his memory forever.

Bailey pulled away after a glorious few seconds and chuckled. Beckett did, too.

THE BACKSTAGERS AND THE FINAL BLACKOUT

When the lights hanging above them began to flicker, Beckett wondered if he might be about to faint, but when he heard the other students reacting to the malfunction, he knew that it wasn't all in his head. Bailey looked around at the sputtering, flashing bulbs. Suddenly, the lights blacked out completely, cloaking the glittering dance floor in total darkness.

✂

Down in the Club Room, Jory, Hunter, Aziz, Adrienne, Sasha, and Reo happily loosened their constricting bow ties and removed their painful dress shoes.

Totally unknown to the rest of the student body of St. Genesius, the Club Room was a place where the Backstagers could be totally themselves. It was an epic theater-nerd cave, packed with artifacts from Genesius shows past, the walls covered in graffiti from all the Backstagers who had come before. As fun as it was to play dress-up for one night, they all knew that in this safe space, the real party was about to begin.

Just as Sasha got the beat-up little radio in the corner to awaken from its slumber and play some music, the door swung open to reveal two beaming seniors.

"Timothy! Jamie!" Hunter cheered.

"I had a feeling you kids would be down here!" Jamie said. He'd tamed his normally unruly long, brown hair into a tight bun and had trimmed his bushy beard for the occasion.

"Dang, Jamie, lookin' sharp!" Jory said as he and Hunter sunk into an ancient couch.

"Isn't he, though?" Timothy said. He'd slicked his long blond hair back, accentuating his angular face. He gave Jamie an affectionate kiss on the cheek. "For stage managers, I do think we clean up nice!"

"Now, who wants bubbles?" Timothy said as he made his way toward the refrigerator in the corner of the room.

"Um, what do you mean?" Hunter asked, ever the caretaker of the group.

"A rare vintage I've been saving for tonight, to celebrate!"

Timothy opened the refrigerator door and pulled out a two-liter bottle of a clear soda with a very retro-looking label.

"Oh my gosh," Aziz marveled. "Is that . . ."

"Crystal Pepsi. Discontinued since 1994!" Timothy said.

"I thought you were kidding about that," Jamie said, shaking his head.

"If that still bubbles," Jory said, "I will be even more terrified of what happens to us if we drink it."

"It's most definitely a cursed beverage," Reo said, eyebrow cocked.

"Oh come on, guys," Timothy said as he started filling plastic cups with the miraculously still-fizzy beverage. "Live a little! We're toasting the end of a spectacular season AND some pretty big news that Jamie and I have to share with you all."

"You're getting MARRIED?!" Sasha leaped up from a beanbag and toppled right to the floor again.

". . . Erm, no," Timothy said. "The big news is, we were both accepted to Wolverine University!"

"You GUYS!" Hunter said, jumping up to embrace them. "Your first-choice school! That's incredible!"

"It's pretty amazing," Timothy said. "I mean, it's a great school, of course, but what I'm most excited about is that we'll get to experience it together."

". . . Totally!" Jamie agreed, though some of the light dimmed in his eyes.

The Backstagers each took a cup of the ancient soda and formed a circle.

"Adrienne, what's the sign for 'Cheers'?" Aziz asked.

"It's *very* difficult," Adrienne said as she raised her cup high and smiled.

Everyone laughed.

"To Timothy and Jamie!" Hunter said. "The two best stage managers St. Genesius ever had. And the best Wolverines that there will ever be!"

The Backstagers all whooped and cheered.

"And to the Backstagers who take up our legacy after we leave," Timothy said. "We raised you well. I know that no matter what happens, you all can handle it. To the Backstagers!"

"TO THE BACKSTAGERS!"

Just as they raised their cups, the lights in the room began to flicker on and off.

"What the heck?" Aziz said. "Power short from the dance?"

"No way," Sasha replied. "I juiced the lights upstairs with a power crystal from the backstage. It should be plenty."

He stepped toward a bare lightbulb that hung in the center of the room that blinked off and on frenetically. A vague shape was beginning to materialize inside the glass. Gazing into the bulb, Sasha said, "You guys . . . it's . . . Phoebe!"

The Backstagers exchanged a worried look and gathered around to see for themselves.

"*Who?*" Adrienne asked Aziz in ASL.

"*Phoebe Murphy,*" he replied.

Adrienne's heart dropped because, of course, Phoebe Murphy was the ghost who haunted the backstage. She lived in the Arch Theater at the heart of the backstage, where all theater magic came from, protecting the backstage and all of its treasures. For her to reach out to them from her peaceful watch could only mean danger.

And, indeed, in the space where its filament should be, there was now the spectral face of a young girl, her hair in pom-poms. She was mouthing something, a silent plea from inside the bulb.

"What is she saying? I can't tell," Reo said.

"I can," Adrienne said, reading her lips. "She's saying, 'Help me'!"

CHAPTER 2

THE BACKSTAGERS CHANGED FROM THEIR FORMAL WEAR TO THEIR CREW blacks as quickly as they could and made their way through the Unsafe door at the back of the Club Room.

As soon as they stepped across its boundary, they entered into another world, the world of the backstage, where theater magic was real—living, breathing, and dangerous.

The Backstagers had passed down the secrets of this magical world to each new generation who passed through their stage doors, and thus, when it was in danger, it was up to the Backstagers to protect it, even if that meant cutting short the most celebratory night of their high school lives.

They raced through the tunnels, the starry maze between the specialized rooms that housed the elements of theater, toward a set of double doors labeled THE GREENROOM.

They passed through the double doors and the galactic darkness of the tunnels gave way to a perfect sunny day in a vast, grassy field. The Greenroom was a special hub that Jory and Reo had created together. Each of the doors that stood in a row along the edges of the field were labeled according to their destination: the Prop Room, the Paint Room, and so on. Tonight, they headed for the very last door in the row, which was labeled VERY UNSAFE. When they reached it, Hunter looked to *his* crew to make sure they were ready for whatever they might face inside. Everyone nodded solemnly.

The Very Unsafe door was labeled as such because beyond it lay the Arch Theater, the most unsafe place in all of the backstage. It was the very heart of all theater magic, where time became nonlinear, creativity became instantly manifest, and literally anything could happen.

It had become a bit less scary when the Backstagers befriended Phoebe and convinced her to guard it from less benevolent spirits, but now they feared that something had come along that even Phoebe couldn't keep away on her own.

They were perhaps most concerned about a secret Phoebe guarded there: the Backstagers' collection of legendary theater artifacts, tools of unrivaled power that were the very building blocks of theater itself. If Phoebe was in danger, so were the artifacts. And if those got into the wrong hands, there was no telling what would happen next.

When they had all passed through the Very Unsafe door, the Backstagers found themselves on the stage of the Arch Theater, where Phoebe held a scepter over her head. The bare light bulb at its end cast a sphere of bluish white light all around her. At the edge of the sphere of light, a figure bashed against the light with a hammer, but the hammer smacked off of the edge of the sphere as if it were solid.

With every forceful bash, the sphere of light flickered but did not go out.

"Phoebe!" Sasha called out to the ghost. "We're here to rescue you!"

"Hey, you there! Stop that right now!" Hunter commanded to the figure.

The figure stopped his pummeling and looked up toward the Backstagers. His face was hidden by a stone mask, an ancient face contorted in a wail of tragedy.

"Thiasos," Jory whispered, because this was the signature mask of the evil organization determined to gather all of the legendary theater artifacts. After being kidnapped by the organization earlier in the year, Jory knew their masks all too well. However, as the figure turned back toward the sphere of light, Jory saw that this mask was actually slightly different than the ones worn by a regular Thiasos soldier, for on the back of his head there was another face with a twisted comedian's smile.

The figure dropped the hammer, then reached into a small pouch on a bulky leather tool belt that hung at his waist. Jory gasped when the figure then pulled, impossibly, an entire sledgehammer out of the pouch.

The figure turned and stared for a moment through his stone eyes at the Backstagers, who still stood clustered at the back wall of the stage. Then, he resumed his assault on the sphere, which flickered more violently with each hit from the massive hammer.

"NO!" Jory cried, making a dash toward the figure at the edge of the stage. Hunter grabbed him, stopping his advance.

"Jory, are you crazy?! That's a sledgehammer! You could get hurt!"

"Well, there's only one of him and there are eight of us! We go together!"

Jory looked desperately to his friends.

Sasha stepped forward and nodded. "We go together!"

With a battle cry, the crowd of Backstagers charged toward the masked invader.

The figure paused his hammering once again and reached back to his tool belt, unclipping a small box that hung off his hip. The masked figure tossed the box toward the encroaching Backstagers, and as the box sprung open, a second masked soldier leaped out from it, stopping the Backstagers in their tracks.

They gasped. How could a fully grown person fit inside a box that was only a few square inches? There was no time to think about that, however, because a third soldier jumped out of the box and stood defiantly before the stunned Backstagers. Then a fourth. Then a fifth.

As more and more Thiasos soldiers emerged from the

box to form a human barrier, the double-faced assailant dropped his sledgehammer and reached into the pouch on his belt again. The figure pulled out a motorized jackhammer and placed the tip to the edge of the sphere of light.

"Uh-oh," was all Aziz could say.

The jackhammer roared on, sending sparks flying off of the flickering sphere of light, which seemed like it could shatter at any moment. The line of guards, now numbering more than ten, began to move toward the terrified Backstagers.

Timothy looked up to Phoebe, whose Ghost Light flashed and began to dim. "What do we do?!" he asked.

"RUN!" she commanded.

The line of Thiasos guards began to run toward the Backstagers, who had no choice but to retreat back through the Very Unsafe door.

They made it through the door and slammed it shut behind them, locking it. The peaceful quiet of the sunny Greenroom was soon broken by the sound of fists pounding against the door from the other side.

"How did they find the Arch Theater?!" Reo asked, his back against the door. "How did they even know to look there?"

"I don't know," Jory said. "I thought the artifacts would be safe there." It had been his idea to store the artifacts in the Arch Theater, and he sounded utterly defeated now.

The pounding from the other side of the door stopped suddenly.

"They stopped," Aziz told Adrienne.

"Is that a good thing?" she asked.

"I'm not so sure," he replied.

And then the bright sun hanging above the Greenroom plunged below the horizon and the whole room was completely dark. Jory screamed. Adrienne took Aziz's hand. Just as suddenly, the sun returned to its position, revealing terrified looks on the Backstagers' faces.

"They have the Master Switch," Sasha said.

"Which means they overpowered the Ghost Light," Reo said.

"They have all of them," Hunter said ominously.

"BACKSTAGERS OF GENESIUS, LISTEN WELL," a roaring voice echoed across the whole field. Adrienne looked to Aziz for a translation, but he couldn't sign while clutching his ears to muffle the sound. All the other Backstagers had their ears covered, too, so it was clear that the Thiasos soldiers must be communicating using the God Mic.

"YOU HAVE LOST. WE HAVE THE GHOST LIGHT, MASTER SWITCH, GOD MIC, AND DESIGNER'S NOTEBOOK. WE DON'T NEED OR WANT ANYTHING ELSE FROM YOU AND WE DON'T WANT TO HURT YOU. STAY

OUT OF THE BACKSTAGE FOR YOUR OWN GOOD. THIS
IS YOUR FINAL WARNING."

Jory turned to the group and said, "We have to get out
of here right now."

"No," Aziz said, "we have to get the artifacts back! Why
would we run just because they said to?"

"Because I drew this room in the Designer's Notebook,
remember?" Jory said. "And anything drawn in the Notebook can be—"

Before he could finish, the Very Unsafe door that they
had just passed through vanished, leaving behind a strange
rectangle of blank whiteness.

"ERASED!"

One by one, each of the doors that lined the edges of
the field disappeared. The Backstagers sprinted as fast as
they could toward the double doors on the other side of the
Greenroom while a massive streak of white cut across
the blue sky above them. Stroke by stroke, it spread until the
entire sky was replaced with vast white nothing.

They were almost at the exit when the grass below Jory's
feet vanished in a swipe. He screamed as he tumbled backward into the nothingness, but Hunter's hand grasped Jory's
just as he was about to be swallowed into the white void.
Jory looked up at him, terrified, as he dangled above a blank
white eternity. Hunter used all of his strength to pull Jory

back onto the solid ground, but there was no time for Jory to thank him for saving his life—the ground all around them was disappearing rapidly.

Leaping over fresh streaks of whiteness as they appeared, the team managed to reach the double doors, bursting through them back into the tunnel and landing in a heap. The double doors slammed shut before vanishing altogether. Where there had moments ago been the Greenroom, there was now just more of the indistinct darkness of the tunnels. The Greenroom was gone forever.

"Are we all okay?" Timothy asked his crew, panting. He scanned the group. Jory, Hunter, Aziz, Reo, Sasha, Adrienne, and Jamie all looked deeply shaken but were thankfully unharmed.

"Let's get back to the Club Room," Jamie said. "We aren't safe back here."

✕

When they slumped through the Unsafe door, Beckett leaped up from the ratty sofa where he'd been waiting for them.

"THERE you guys are! They had to call off the rest of the dance due to technical problems. I tried to help, but we couldn't figure it out," he said. He then noticed their somber expressions and asked, "What were you doing in the backstage? And why are you out of your tuxes?"

"The artifacts," Hunter said, depleted. "They're gone."

". . . What?" Beckett sat back down.

"It was Thiasos," Jory said. "They'd sent a soldier. Or a small army of soldiers. Phoebe was warning us with the lights."

"No," Beckett whispered.

"We'll explain everything," Timothy said. "You all told your parents that we're going out for burgers at the Hand Jive, right? That buys us a little time to debrief and make a plan."

"But Bailey is waiting upstairs with the Penitent girls for us to get those very burgers," Beckett said. "What do I tell *her*?"

"You're gonna have to make something up, Beck," Aziz said.

"No, no, I can't! She'll be devastated."

"Beckett, Thiasos has all of our artifacts," Jamie said, taking Beckett's shoulders. "All of them, do you understand?"

"I just thought we could take one night off from all of this," Beckett said, defeated. The Backstagers shared a pitiful look. After a moment, he sighed. "I'll be right back."

☒

"Oh . . . oh my gosh, what did you all eat?!" Bailey asked.

She and Beckett stood in front of the school as cars snaked their way around the parking lot, whisking the students away from the awkward dancing and toward comfier clothes, fattening food, and friendly hangs.

"We, uh, we had some bean dip while we were getting ready," Beckett lied. "Maybe it was the lettuce—I feel like they're recalling lettuce, like, every day now."

"Totally," Bailey said. She wore a mask of empathetic concern, but Beckett could tell that she was seriously bummed out.

"Yeah, I honestly don't know how I was spared but the Club Room is like a war zone right now. There's only one bathroom down there and it's very old and—"

"I get it, Beck. Don't need the visual."

"Right. Sorry. Anyway, I'm thinking burgers are like, not ideal right now."

"Yeah, maybe not."

"So . . . I guess I'll just catch up with you tomorrow."

"Okay. I guess I'll just head home." Bailey's eyes sunk to the ground and Beckett felt the worst he'd ever felt in his life. Just then, thankfully, Adrienne appeared and wrapped her arm around Bailey's shoulder.

"I'm assuming Beckett told you about Pukefest. Man, I have never seen a color like that come out of a human body!"

"Ugh, please spare me!" Bailey laughed. Beckett was relieved to see her smile.

"Anyway," Adrienne said, "I don't know how I still have any appetite at all after what these eyes have seen, but I'm still down for burgers if you are, Bailey. All the Penitent girls are going. Come so we can compare notes on these boys' dance moves!"

Bailey chuckled and said, "Okay, take care of your crew, Beck. I'll text you tomorrow. I had a really nice time."

"Me too!" Beckett said. "Really, like the best time ever. I'm really sorry."

"It happens," Bailey said. They stood there awkwardly a moment.

". . . Well, bye," Beckett said, finally.

"Night," Bailey said as she and Adrienne headed for their ride.

Beckett watched her go. He couldn't believe that only a half hour ago they were on the dance floor, on top of the world, and now he was here, feeling about as high as a sea slug on the bottom of the ocean. Still, his crew needed him more than Bailey did right now. He took a deep, cleansing breath and made his way back into the school. It was going to be a long night.

CHAPTER 3

THE BACKSTAGERS HAD PERFORMED THE RITUAL ONCE BEFORE, and with so much on their minds, they gathered the necessary materials in the Club Room almost automatically.

A circle of chalk on the floor.

A lit white candle.

A bowl of sea salt.

A glass of spring water.

A swirl of incense smoke.

"Hey, guys," Hunter said. "Everybody turn your phones off. They have the God Mic again and could be listening to us through them. From now on, let's only turn them on when we absolutely need to."

The Backstagers nodded and powered down.

When they were all seated inside the circle of chalk, Reo

called out, "Phoebe Murphy! Are you there?! We need to speak with you urgently!"

Hunter, Jory, Timothy, Jamie, Sasha, and Aziz all bowed their heads and focused their minds on Phoebe, benevolent ghost of the Arch Theater. They'd learned the hard way to be very specific about who they were contacting when attempting to converse with spirits.

"Phoebe, appear to us, please!" Reo commanded. The flame in the candle flickered.

"I'm here." A small voice echoed all around them.

The Backstagers raised their heads and watched the incense smoke solidify slightly in the air. There was the figure of a girl. Two signature pom-poms in her hair. And suddenly the face of Phoebe Murphy, a vision made of smoke and candlelight.

"Phoebe! You're okay!" Reo said.

"I'm unharmed—I am a ghost, after all," Phoebe said. "But 'okay' is another story. The artifacts have been stolen. I'm sorry I couldn't do more to protect them."

"You did your best," Jory said. "That soldier, that . . . Double-face. His tools were incredible."

"Yeah, how was he doing that?" Aziz asked. "He pulled a freaking jackhammer out of that tiny pouch on his belt!"

"And the box," Sasha said. "He fit a whole entourage in there."

"I did wonder what kind of tool could defeat the power of a legendary artifact," Phoebe echoed.

"You don't mean . . ." Timothy looked to his crew.

"Those were *other* legendary artifacts," Jamie said. "What were the other artifacts Mr. Rample told us about?"

Hunter took inventory. "We know about the Ghost Light, Master Switch, God Mic, and Designer's Notebook. Then there was . . . the Carpenter's Belt . . . the Prop Box—"

"A belt and a box!" Jory said. "That must have been them."

"That means," Jory said, gravely, "with our four artifacts combined with the two they brought to steal them, they have six of the seven."

Everything was silent except for the licking of the candle's flame. Thiasos had told Jory that they were aiming to collect all seven artifacts, and now they were dangerously close to their goal.

"So what artifact does that leave?!" Aziz asked.

"It's called . . . the Show Bible," Hunter said. "That was the seventh artifact Rample named."

"Then we have to find it," Aziz said, always looking to fix what was broken. "It's our only hope."

"But how?" Sasha asked. "Before, I could have used the Master Switch to light our way to it, but now Thiasos has it. I bet they're on their way to the Show Bible right now!"

Jory nodded and said, "And even if we could somehow

cut them off on their way, they have six artifacts to fight us with. We wouldn't stand a chance!"

"And the Greenroom is erased," Reo said. "Now all the rooms are scattered throughout the tunnels again. If we can't even find our way back to the Arch Theater, where do we start looking?"

"Wait a minute," Jory said. "Reo, how did we find all those rooms in the first place?"

"Oh . . ." Reo said.

"What do you mean?" Timothy asked.

"The backstage responds to the will of the Backstager, right?" Jory said. "If you need to find a room badly enough, it will show itself to you. Reo found a way to focus his will on specific rooms so we could find them and catalogue them in the Greenroom. Reo, if you can do it to find rooms, maybe you can do it to find the Show Bible?!"

"In theory, it would work, but I don't know . . ." Reo said. "The rooms were all places we'd been before. The Show Bible has to be much better hidden in the backstage."

"Well, it's worth a try, right?" Aziz insisted.

"It will take some deep meditation, but yes," Reo said.

"There is one bit of good news," Jamie said. "Next Friday is the start of finals week. Timothy and I will have to be taking tests with the other seniors, but you guys will have the whole week to search the backstage, uninterrupted."

"Just hurry," Phoebe warned. "I can protect the Arch Theater without the Ghost Light for a time, but if any truly powerful entities try to move in, I'll be defenseless."

"And I don't know why Thiasos is trying to gather the artifacts," Jory said, "but I don't want to find out. When I was their prisoner, Aleka talked about using them all to summon a great power. I doubt they want to use that power to put on a stellar show."

"Our best hope is to find the Show Bible, then, and keep it hidden," Aziz said.

"Speaking of keeping it hidden," Hunter said, "we still don't know how Thiasos found our hiding place in the Arch Theater. That was the safest place in all of the backstage."

"It's a mystery," Phoebe said, her image growing fainter. "One I suggest you solve, and fast. Hurry, Backstagers! Find the Show Bible before Thiasos does!"

As her spectral voice rang out, a draft picked up out of nowhere in the Club Room and extinguished the candle and the incense, leaving the Backstagers in quiet darkness.

CHAPTER 4

THE FLAMBEAU Online Edition, Monday
Special Breaking News Report by Quentin
Quackenbush, Student Editor in Chief

Sources close to three different faculty members are reporting new details about today's surprise school-wide assembly. While the weekend
was awash with rumors that senior pranksters
caused the electrical troubles that derailed the
Dance at the Gym last Friday night, some students
suspect a much darker problem (pun intended).

"This is way, way bigger than some flickering
lights," one such student, whose name is being
withheld for fear of disciplinary action, told the
Flambeau. In text messages sent directly to the

student editing staff, the source provided information regarding phone calls they overheard while studying near the faculty lounge. The source described the calls as "desperate" pleas from a "top-ranking" faculty member for funds to keep the school afloat.

Could the dramatic light show at the Dance at the Gym be the result of delinquent bills rather than delinquent students?

We will all learn the truth together, just after lunch period, when we gather in the St. Genesius auditorium . . .

Beckett closed the tab on his phone and said, "Should I send an anonymous tip that the electrical problems were actually caused by a ghost trying to warn some Backstagers about an evil, two-faced villain stealing some ancient powerful objects?" He drained the last of his Diet Coke, the fifth he'd had that day.

Hunter chuckled and said, "Even with a story that enticing, I can't imagine Quentin Quackenbush publishing the truth."

They were sitting together in the crowded St. Genesius lunchroom, practically shouting over the din of hundreds of other students furiously speculating about the surprise assembly that had been called. It's true that the early whisper was that a few seniors had sabotaged the lighting at the dance as a prank, but now the *Flambeau* scoop had turned that speculation on its head.

"And speaking of the truth," Hunter said, "how are things with Bailey?"

"I think we're okay. I just hate that I had to lie to her," Beckett said.

"Well you know, Beck, you could just tell her everything."

"Definitely not."

"How come? Literally all of her friends are Backstagers! We're all caught up in this except for her."

"Maybe that's good. Maybe I wanna protect her from it."

Hunter scrunched his face up. "Protect her? I don't think Bailey is the kind of person who needs protecting."

"No," Beckett said, "I don't mean protect *her*, I mean protect . . . us. She's the only thing I have in my life that's separate from the backstage. I love the way I can shut all that off when I'm with her and we can just be . . ."

"Normal," Hunter said, nodding.

"Yeah. And I'm afraid if I tell her, show her *everything*, she might run. The backstage is a lot to put on a person."

"You're telling me," Hunter said. There was something far away in his eyes, but as he opened his mouth to say more, Jory plopped down beside him with a tray of cheese fries.

"If Genesius really is going under, I hope these fries survive the budget cuts," Jory said. "They sustain me."

He scooped a glob of neon orange cheese onto a fry and offered it to Hunter as Aziz, Sasha, and Reo rejoined the table with snacks.

"It feels so strange," Aziz said, "to just be carrying on like everything is fine. Eating cheese fries and soft pretzels while Thiasos is out there with our artifacts."

"Finals week starts Friday," Hunter said. "That's when we can all get to work looking for the Show Bible."

"You mean *I* can get to work . . ." Reo said, looking overwhelmed at the thought.

"We'll all be there to support you however we can," Hunter said.

The bell sounded, and suddenly it was time to learn what awaited them at the assembly.

✂

The cafeteria had been a cacophony of gossip, but the auditorium was an absolute roar as the entire student body swapped theories about what was about to go down.

As underclassmen, the Backstagers took a row of seats in the back. Hunter locked eyes with Timothy, who was hauling a podium to the center of the stage with Jamie. Timothy shrugged, just as mystified by the urgent assembly.

After adjusting the microphone on the podium and

switching it on, Timothy and Jamie cleared the stage and soon, after the toll of a bell signaled the beginning of the period, it was time.

As Ms. LuPone, headmaster of St. Genesius, stepped into the stage lights and made her way to the podium, the hundreds of students fell silent and the room was instead filled with palpable tension. Ms. LuPone adjusted the microphone, clearing her throat, and then looked up to the sea of expectant faces.

"Good afternoon, students. My apologies for interrupting your classes today, especially with exams approaching, but as our year draws to a close, I wanted to make everyone aware that next year is going to be a little different. My great-grandfather founded this school with the intention of providing the highest-quality education at a tuition cost that would be accessible to all students—"

She paused, emotion catching in her throat. Jory looked at Hunter. *This doesn't sound good.*

". . . And I am very proud that we have been able to provide that to thousands of students over the years. Unfortunately, we can no longer make ends meet while keeping tuition the same. The board wanted me to raise tuition, but I couldn't imagine betraying my great-grandfather's vision for the school, so I'm afraid . . . we have to take another option."

There were whispers in the audience.

A sophomore boy stood and shouted, "So Genesius is closing down?! Where will we all go?!"

Jory's heart sank. In this short year, Genesius had become a home for him, and the Backstagers, his family.

"No, no of course not!" Ms. LuPone replied, quieting the murmurs. "There was a miracle at the last minute! An investor agreed to buy the school, pay off our debts, and even upgrade all of our facilities while keeping tuition exactly as is. So next year, the only difference for you will be newer and better everything. And a different headmaster. But that's okay!" she said, smiling through misty eyes. "All good things must come to an end, and it has been the honor of my life, serving you students. I am overjoyed, really, that the wonderful Thiasos Organization has come in to save the day."

The Backstagers gasped. Aziz stood, ready to charge the stage. He didn't really know what he would do when he got up there, but Aziz was the type to leap before he looked. Hunter, more strategic, pulled him back into his seat. They shared a grave look.

"It is my pleasure," Ms. LuPone continued, "to introduce the president of the Thiasos Organization, Mrs. Thiasos herself!"

Ms. LuPone stepped to the side of the podium and

banged her hands together in applause as if her sheer enthusiasm would spread to the entire student body and make everything all right.

A woman entered from the wings to replace her at the podium. She was tall and thin with a stark white suit, heels, and gleaming short hair—also white and immaculately quaffed. To the untrained eye, she appeared a polished, even glamorous figure who moved with power and purpose—an ideal new leader for a struggling school. However, the Backstagers knew that anyone with her last name couldn't be bringing good news.

"Good afternoon, students!" Even her Mediterranean accent was alluring. "And thank you, Ms. LuPone, for that wonderful introduction. My company, the Thiasos Organization, saw that your school was struggling and decided that it was far too special to close down. We are honored to continue the work that the LuPone family began generations ago while updating the school for a new generation! We want to begin the next school year with fresh facilities, but we have quite a lot of work to do before then, so do forgive our dust as we start work immediately! In fact, we are beginning with the renovation of this very auditorium!"

The back doors of the auditorium swung open, and two lines of construction workers in white THIASOS branded uniforms and hard hats entered and walked down the two aisles toward the lip of the stage. Sasha looked up at one of them as he passed by and he sneered back.

Mrs. Thiasos leaned into the microphone, her eyes gleaming with dark delight, and practically sang, "And of course, we'll be renovating the *theater* as well."

Jory took Hunter's hand and Hunter squeezed. They were powerless.

"Yes," Mrs. Thiasos cooed, "next year, St. Genesius will be able to boast a state-of-the-art theater facility, and I am very pleased to announce to our Drama Club students out there that the Thiasos Organization will even provide a professional stage crew!"

The students cheered, but the Backstagers sat frozen as Mrs. Thiasos flashed her twisted smile.

CHAPTER 5

AS THRONGS OF STUDENTS POURED OUT OF THE AUDITORIUM chatting gleefully about what improvements they'd like to see made to the school over summer vacation—"Soft-serve machines!" "A hot tub!" "VR lounge!"—Timothy and Jamie ran up the aisles to intercept their stricken crew.

"You guys okay?" Timothy asked as he wrapped Sasha in a hug.

"We had no idea," Jamie said. "They're already back there, the workers. They padlocked the stage door shut."

"So how do we get to the Club Room?" Hunter asked.

"And the *backstage*?" Reo added. "How can I search for the Show Bible with no access to the backstage?"

Timothy and Jamie just looked at each other sadly. They didn't have an answer.

"Ah, just who I wanted to see," cooed a voice.

The Backstagers turned to see Mrs. Thiasos striding up the aisle toward them, smiling her marionette smile as Ms. LuPone scurried along behind her.

"Yes," said Ms. LuPone. "These are our Genesius Backstagers!"

"*Were*," Aziz said, coldly. Ms. LuPone's smile fell.

"I expected you might be . . . concerned about the announcement," Mrs. Thiasos said. "But fear not! This will be a great opportunity for you! We will be hiring the finest professional crew possible, and I will personally see to it that each of you gets an apprenticeship to learn from them."

Ms. LuPone looked eagerly at the Backstagers, whose stony faces did not ease her anxiety.

"They will help you learn all about crewing out in the real world," Mrs. Thiasos said. "And I expect you can, in turn, help them learn about the ins and outs of this particular space. I'm sure there will be some . . . artifacts . . . of the old system left behind. Maybe we can all help each other. What is it you say here in this country: 'If you can't beat them, join them'?"

"We'll think about it," Jory said, though his eyes told her exactly what he thought about it already.

"I hope you do," she replied with a stare icier than her whiteout outfit.

THE BACKSTAGERS AND THE FINAL BLACKOUT

✕

Out in the student lot, the Backstagers circled up.

"We'll . . . come up with something," Timothy said.

"We always do," Jamie agreed, though he didn't sound very inspired.

"Like what?" Aziz said, agitated. "Our artifacts are gone, our access to the backstage is gone! We lost!"

"Maybe Penitent Angels?" Sasha suggested. "All the backstages are connected! We can use their Unsafe door?"

"When, though?" Beckett asked. "We'd have to, like, sneak in after-hours and keep coming up with excuses for our parents."

"I don't know if I'll be able to do my thing under that kind of pressure," Reo confessed.

"What do you think, Hunter?" Jory asked.

"Um . . ." Hunter's eyes were fixed on the pavement. "I do have one idea. It might be a little . . . controversial."

"What is it?!" Timothy asked.

"We stop," Hunter said, finally looking up to his friends.

"What? What do you mean?" Timothy said.

"I mean we stop . . . fighting. Aziz is right, they have everything we've been using to fight back. The game is over, and honestly? I'm not really sure if I want to play anymore."

He turned to Jory, who looked at his boyfriend as if Hunter were a stranger.

"Jory, back in the Greenroom, you almost got erased. Do you understand what that would have meant? You would have *died*, Jory. And this is after you were kidnapped by Thiasos once before. After we all got lost in the Arch Theater and nearly got eaten by echo spiders and, heck, after we *DID* die fighting the Arch Ghost! We put ourselves in so much danger all the time and I don't really know what we have to show for it. Nobody knows. Nobody thanks us."

"It's not about being *thanked*," Jory said.

"What I mean is, I don't even know exactly what we're fighting for or against, but I know we put ourselves at incredible risk doing it. What if Thiasos does get all the artifacts? What's the worst thing that could happen? Do you think it's worth dying over? I'm actually asking."

Hunter looked around the circle and all of the Backstagers were quiet.

All except for Jory, who said, "I don't know what their goal is, but I can't un-know what I *do* know about the backstage and the artifacts. Can you really just go back to putting on shows and only worrying about where to sit at lunch and what grade you're getting on a test?"

"It doesn't sound so bad, honestly," Hunter said. "It sounds normal."

"But we're not normal," Jory said. "We're Backstagers. It's unfair and it's scary and it's sometimes a burden, but it's *our* burden and for me . . ." His voice broke a bit as some tears welled up. "For me, it's the most special thing in my life. And I'm not just going to give it up because some *corporation* tried to take it."

Hunter nodded, his eyes misting over as well.

"And as for people looking out for us . . ." Jory continued. "We look out for each other. Maybe ninety-nine percent of St. Genesius doesn't know who we are or what we do for them, but I know how you've saved the world this year, Hunter. And you, Sasha. And you, Beckett. And Aziz. And Timothy. And Jamie. And even Reo, in just a short time. You might not believe in yourselves right now, but I'll believe in you, always. And I hope you'll believe in me, too. Because we're a crew."

CHAPTER 6

USUALLY, WHEN JORY ARRIVED HOME, THE HOUSE WAS VERY QUIET. His mom worked long hours starting very early in the morning, so he'd often come home to find some dinner on the table, the TV softly playing some uncomplicated sitcom, and his mom asleep in her chair, still in her work clothes.

Tonight, Jory was surprised to hear his mom laughing and socializing as he opened his front door. He was downright shocked when he swung it open and saw the man who was making his mom laugh so jovially.

"Mr. Rample?!" Jory said, looking at the former faculty advisor of the Backstagers like he'd seen a ghost.

"Jory, my boy!" Mr. Rample practically leaped up from the sofa, impressive for someone who'd put as many years into the theater as he had, and scooped Jory into a hug.

"What are you doing here?"

"Well, right now, I'm enjoying the heck out of your mom's company and delicious corn-cranberry cookies! You're a lucky kid!"

"You want another one? Or do you want to save room for dinner? We're doing taco night!" Jory's mom asked, blushing.

"Kind of you, ma'am, but I came to talk business and I'd better stick to it."

"Business?" Jory asked.

"Mr. Rample has been talking to me about an opportunity for you during exams week," Jory's mom said.

"That is, if you weren't planning on spending it glued to the couch, binging TV! I wouldn't blame you!" Mr. Rample said.

"What is it?" Jory asked, feeling the first bit of hope he'd felt in days.

"Well, ever since my time at Genesius, I've been crewing at a regional theater a few hours away in the country: the Forest of Arden Theater. It just so happens that we're going into tech for our production of *Tiny Store of Terrors* this weekend, and I was wondering if you and the guys wanted to come spend your week off with us, shadowing the professional Backstagers and lending a hand with the tech?"

Jory could have cried in that moment. To shadow at a professional theater was an amazing opportunity on its own, but coming at this moment, it was an even greater one—the chance to get back into the backstage.

"Oh, Mr. Rample, I'd love to! It's okay, Mom?"

"It sounds a lot nicer than that excursion to Greece," she said, "whatever that was all about."

"You know, ma'am," Mr. Rample said, "I think I will take you up on one more of those cookies, if it's no trouble."

"No trouble at all," Jory's mom said, beaming. She made her way into the kitchen, and as soon as she was out of the room, Jory launched into action.

"Mr. Rample," he whispered, "you have no idea how lucky this is. There's this organization called Thias—"

"Is your phone off?" Mr. Rample asked urgently. "Remember, they have the God Mic now, they could be listening to any of this."

"It is, yeah," Jory said, stunned that Rample was one step ahead of him.

"Hunter has been updating me on the whole Thiasos saga," Mr. Rample explained. "We'll leave Friday morning, and you guys will have uninterrupted backstage time until the end of exams week. It's not long, but hopefully it's enough time to find the Show Bible, recover the other artifacts, and defeat Thiasos, once and for all."

"That's . . . a lot," Jory said.

"If anyone can do it, it's the Backstagers of Genesius." Mr. Rample smiled encouragingly at Jory, who nodded in agreement. It was a shot in the dark, but at least it was a shot.

⋊

Beckett wasn't sure how long he'd been lying on his bed, staring at the ceiling, when the ring of his house phone broke his trance. It had been a hard couple of days, and he was feeling numb and depleted. When he heard his dad shout, "Beckett, it's for you!" though, he bolted upright, suddenly a person again. He ran down the stairs to the family landline. Maybe it was Hunter or Timothy or one of the other guys with some news. He took the receiver from his dad and said, "Hello?"

"There you are," Bailey said on the other end. Beckett's heart began to race.

"Bailey! Oh! Hey! What's up?"

"I've been texting you all afternoon! And when I called, it went straight to voicemail." She laughed. "I had to, like, use the phone book to get your family's landline number. Very old-timey."

Crap, Beckett thought. His mind had been racing ever since the assembly, so it never occurred to him that Bailey might be trying to call.

"Oh . . . gosh, I'm sorry, I came home and totally crashed." He winced as the lie escaped his lips.

"Ah . . . okay," Bailey said with a sigh.

". . . Is it okay?" Beckett asked, hearing her tone.

"Well, I mean yeah, I just haven't heard from you much since Dance at the Gym. I had to hear about Genesius getting bought from Adrienne. I thought you would have told me."

"I . . . I guess I'm still just in shock."

"I'm just worried—I mean . . . at the dance . . . did I move too fast? I thought we were ready, but then you went to find the guys and suddenly the after-party was canceled and, I dunno, I felt like maybe I scared you off."

Beckett's heart fell into his shoes.

"Oh my gosh, no!" he said. "No, I was so, so happy! Am so happy! Just bad timing with the . . . um . . . I mean, you know, with the—"

"Food poisoning?" Bailey didn't sound convinced.

"Right!" Beckett said. This is why he wasn't an Onstager;

he was a terrible actor. "Yeah, just really, really, cosmically crappy timing. I promise."

"Well that's good," Bailey said. "I just had this feeling that there was something you weren't telling me. We've known each other a long time and you've never kept anything from me, so if you were keeping something, it scares me to imagine what that might be."

Beckett swallowed hard, not sure of what to say. Luckily, or unluckily, depending on how you look at it, at that moment, his dad approached.

"Beckett?" he said, "There's someone here to see you."

He gestured behind himself to reveal, to Beckett's utter surprise, Mr. Rample.

"Hey Bailey, I actually gotta go, someone's here."

"Okay."

"I'll call you later tonight, though, okay?"

"Sure, Beckett. Later," Bailey said abruptly and hung up.

He looked down at the phone, not sure that he'd handled that call very well at all, then back up to Mr. Rample.

"Mr. Rample, what's—"

"Sorry to interrupt you, but time is of the essence," Mr. Rample said. "We have plans to discuss."

CHAPTER 7

WHY DON'T WE JUST GO NOW?" AZIZ ASKED. "GET OUR parents to make an excuse and head to Forest of Arden right away. We could be in the backstage by tonight." Aziz was not good at letting a problem go unfixed.

"Thiasos would suspect something if we all took off for vacation early together," Hunter explained. "We have to do this by the book."

Aziz rested his head on the lunchroom table, frustrated. It was only Tuesday, and it was bad enough that they had to sit and spin their wheels until Friday, when exams week began. It was extra bad that, now, they didn't even have the safety of the Club Room to hang in and hatch their plan. They had to gather in the cafeteria with all of the Nonstagers (kids who didn't do theater at all) where any ear might belong to a Thiasos spy.

"Besides," Beckett said, "I have an idea of something we can do to help today."

"What is it?" Aziz asked, raising his head.

"Well, this afternoon is the final Drama Club meeting of the year," Beckett explained. "We have to elect next year's Drama Club president."

"Which will be a Blake and Kevin McQueen ticket," Hunter said. "As always."

It was true, the twins had been the copresidents of the club for all three years of their run at St. Genesius and there was no reason to suspect that their senior year would be any different.

"Are they even speaking, though, after the *Tammy* thing?" Jory asked.

"They always run unopposed, so I doubt it matters," Hunter said.

"My point is," Beckett said, "that at the elections meeting, students can bring up issues they'd like to be addressed in the club next year. I thought we could stand up as the Backstagers and ask the Onstagers to join us in rejecting the professional crew. Maybe it could get us into the backstage sooner."

"I don't know," Reo said. "Do you really think this huge organization is going to listen to the demands of a student group?"

"*If* we can even talk the club into demanding it," Jory added.

"That might actually work out even better for us," Beckett said, "because it would look awfully strange for the new owners of a school to reject a simple student wish to keep an extracurricular club student-operated," Beckett said. "I mean, that would be *super* shady. Then, we could take the issue to the Nonstagers, get the whole school behind us. Maybe expose Thiasos for the shadowy creeps they are. It might make Ms. LuPone think twice about turning the school over to these people while she's still around."

"Honestly, I'm willing to try anything," Aziz said.

"POWER TO THE PEOPLE!" Sasha cried, pretzel crumbs flying from his mouth.

><

That afternoon, the Onstagers and Backstagers all gathered in the auditorium for the Drama Club meeting. There was a strange energy in the room, because this was the first meeting since Blake McQueen had stepped down as director of *Tammy*, and no one was quite sure how the *Tammy* affair had left the twins' relationship.

Everything seemed surprisingly normal, though, when the twins took the stage together, commanding the silence of the room.

"Good afternoon, St. Genesius Drama," Blake said

soberly. "I want to begin by addressing the elephant in the room. Yes, even though I chose to step away from *Tammy* for artistic reasons, I am still your copresident and I wanted to let you know that I saw the production and found it . . . fascinating." There was definitely shade there, but for Blake McQueen, this was about as vulnerable as anyone had ever seen him. "I want to congratulate Beckett on his wonderful work as director, and you all for bringing that work to life onstage and backstage."

Kevin smiled at his brother as the room applauded. Aziz looked to Beckett. Maybe the Drama Club could be a unified front against Thiasos.

"Thank you, Blake," Kevin said. "We're glad to have you back. I know I am . . . Anyway . . ." He looked down and shuffled some notes he was holding, though, knowing Kevin, he was fully off-book for the meeting and actually just needed a moment to compose himself.

"With that behind us," he said, "let's get to the business at hand. Deadline for dues is coming up in a couple of weeks, so please get that in if you haven't. One of our Onstagers has reported his dry shampoo that went missing from the *Tammy* dressing room has still not been returned. He'd like to note that it is *salon grade* and so he'd really appreciate it back. Last, but certainly not least, there's the matter of Drama Club presidency for the fall. For the new kids in the room: Under normal club business, we'd now hear from the candidates, the other students would have the chance to ask questions about policy, and then the candidates would campaign over exams week with an election to follow before the year lets out. However, unless anyone else would like to now announce their candidacy, we can go ahead and vote now and save ourselves the trouble. I suspect there is no . . . opposition?"

He and Blake scanned the crowd of students, all but daring someone to speak up. Beckett took a sip of his Diet Coke for courage and stood up.

"I don't want to run against you guys," he said, "but I do wonder if we can still ask questions about policy. You are still candidates, right?"

Blake's eyes narrowed and he said, "*Unopposed* candidates, but candidates, yes. I suppose that would be appropriate."

"Good," Beckett said. "Because the Backstagers have something to say. Obviously, we think the decision to replace us with a professional crew is ridiculous and insulting. It's not happening with any other student club. We stand by our work this year and we'd like the Onstagers to stand with us and reject the professional crew so that we can keep our positions and ensure that the student Drama Club remains in the control of the students."

THE BACKSTAGERS AND THE FINAL BLACKOUT

There was an affirmative murmur in the audience. The Onstagers and the Backstagers had a historically tense relationship, not unlike a sibling rivalry, but when Beckett directed *Tammy* this year and broke down the walls between the groups, relations improved in a big way. The Backstagers came to respect the artistry of the Onstagers more and, in turn, the Onstagers began to see the Backstagers as a hard-working part of the team, not just the weirdos who worked in the dark to make the Onstagers look good.

Kevin nodded sympathetically and said, "Well, of course. That sounds totally—"

"Impossible," Blake interrupted.

Kevin looked at his brother in shock. Now the auditorium was tittering with tension.

"Uh-oh," Sasha whispered.

"No one is saying that we aren't grateful for the work you all have done," Blake said. "You are all incredibly skilled and we have put on some amazing productions together. However, I can't, as president, turn down the generous offer of professional help just to be kind. My number-one priority is the quality of the Genesius Drama productions."

"Does anyone here think the quality of the productions has been lacking?" Beckett asked the room.

"No!" an Onstager cried. "The Backstagers are amazing!"

"The Rainbow Barricade in *Les Terribles* was Broadway quality," added another.

"So was the lighting in *Lease*!"

"And the sound in *Tammy*."

"Yeah, come through, Backstagers!"

The Onstagers cheered in support. Kevin McQueen leaned toward his brother and whispered, "They're right, Blake. It's not fair to the Backstagers. Surely we can support them."

But Blake cried, "ENOUGH," quieting the room.

"It's not about the quality of the productions *lacking*," he said, "though if I'm completely honest, *Tammy* was not my taste at all. It's about the Thiasos crew being even better. We have a chance to have professional-level productions and if the Backstagers want to stand in the way of that, even as Thiasos is offering them internships to learn from the professionals, well, I find that *selfish*. Besides, if no one is running against us, then I don't know why we're still talking about this. All in favor of the McQueen ticket say—"

"Wait." Kevin interrupted his brother, who glared back at him.

". . . Yes?" Blake hissed.

"My brother, I know our relationship has been strained, and I've been so happy we've been making amends. The last thing I want is to cause more division between us, but

I can't stand for this. If you won't support the Backstagers, then I have no choice but to support them myself . . . in opposition to you."

There was a collective gasp in the audience. Even at an administrative meeting, the McQueens really knew how to amp up the drama.

"What are you *suggesting*?" Blake asked, trying with every cell in his body to remain composed.

"I take no pleasure in announcing that I will not be running for president on a ticket with you, brother, but rather . . . as an individual. As an opposing candidate!"

There were some cheers in the crowd as well as some guffaws.

"Well, dang," Aziz said, impressed.

Blake could only stare at his brother, who looked back mournfully.

Timothy broke the silence and announced, "In that case, elections will be held when we return from exams week. The candidates may use this next week and a half to campaign in any way they see fit. The race is on!"

Blake stormed off, leaving his brother behind. Kevin looked to where the Backstagers were sitting and gave them a nod of solidarity.

"Things are about to get very interesting," Hunter said.

CHAPTER 8

W E ARE ALL ONE CREW.

Kevin McQueen for Drama Club President

The first sign went up the very next morning, a simple hand-drawn expression of unity with the Backstagers.

Sasha admired the sign hanging in one of the hallways on his way to English class. Even though this whole election thing was really the Backstagers' backup plan to resist Thiasos while they waited to depart for the Forest of Arden Theater, he was still moved by the sentiment.

When he emerged from English class fifty minutes later, he was startled to find the sign had been eclipsed by a larger, professionally printed banner.

KEEP THE DRAMA ONSTAGE.

BLAKE MCQUEEN FOR DRAMA CLUB PRESIDENT

But it wasn't until he sat down at lunch period that Sasha saw how divided the Drama Club had really become.

"Check it *out*," Aziz said to Sasha as he pointed toward the Onstagers' table.

There, two Onstager boys, Jay and Will, were locked in a heated, tearful argument. Sasha strained to hear them.

"I can't believe you don't put Onstagers first!" Will cried. "I thought I knew you!"

"Obviously you don't if you think I'm the kind of person who'd leave the Backstagers behind!" Jay replied passionately.

Sasha turned back to Aziz and said, "But they're *the* power showmance of Genesius Drama. If they break up, love must not EXIST!"

Suddenly, there was a crash as Will flipped his tray in frustration, sending disco fries and fruit punch everywhere. He stormed off as Jay sat, shocked, dripping punch and gravy.

Aziz could only shake his head and say, "Politics, man . . ."

✕

The situation became so tense that by the time Friday rolled around, the Backstagers could have easily forgotten that the relief they were feeling was due to getting back to the backstage and not simply getting away from the drama.

They all gathered in the student parking lot of Genesius and loaded Mr. Rample's van with their bags.

Bailey had come by to see them all off. Beckett greeted her with an awkward wave and said, "We're not going to have much service out in the country, so email is probably better than texts or calls for the week. But I promise to check in when I can!"

"That's funny," she said. "I see shows at Forest of Arden with my family all the time and I never have a problem."

"Erm, what I mean is that the guys are all trying to unplug this week. You know, *Tiny Store of Terrors* is such a huge technical show. We don't want any distractions."

"Distractions. Right." Bailey looked down at the pavement.

"No, I just mean—"

"No, I get it, Beck. This is a huge opportunity for you guys. Just . . . check in, okay?"

"I promise."

He smiled at her and she smiled back, though it seemed to take a bit more effort. Beckett leaned forward, but before Bailey realized that he was leaning in for a kiss—or, he *hoped* it was before she'd realized—she spun around and made her way back toward her car, waving to the guys.

"Don't get eaten by any rogue plant puppets!" she said. And then she was gone.

Beckett could scarcely unpack the moment before Sasha asked him, "Hey, Beck, can you give me a hand with my bag? I'm too short!"

The duffel bag was bigger than minuscule Sasha, and as he struggled to hoist it into the back of the van, he looked a bit like a tiny dog lugging a whole fallen tree branch. Beckett had to crack a smile.

"I hope you boys know how ticked off I am that you get to save the world AND hang with the Forest of Arden crew while we have to take tests all week," Timothy said, cramming a backpack onto the top of the pile.

"You make it sound like a vacation," Reo said. Timothy's smile fell a bit.

"Sorry, Reo, I was just kidding. We just really wish we could help you."

"Any idea how you'll start?" Jamie asked.

"I'll perform some divination, ask my spirit guides," Reo replied. "Hopefully they feel like talking."

"That's everything," Mr. Rample said, slamming the van's trunk doors shut. "Ready to head out, Backstagers?"

"Thanks again, Mr. Rample," Timothy said as he and Jamie began hugging their crew goodbye.

"Don't mention it," Mr. Rample said. "Once a Backstager, always a Backstager."

And soon they were off, barreling down a leafy green highway, deeper and deeper into the country.

As Jory looked out the window, he felt freedom and excitement he hadn't felt since he was on the plane to Greece, though this time, it was so much better since he was with his best friends.

"Okay, so what do we know about the Show Bible?" Hunter asked. He was riding shotgun since he was the most senior Backstager without Timothy and Jamie present.

"Well, obviously I don't know about the *legendary* Show Bible," Beckett said, "but 'show bible' is a term stage managers use for the master script of a production. Where they write down all of the blocking and cues and stuff."

"So we think the legendary Show Bible . . . is a script?" Aziz asked.

"Some kind of book, I bet," Beckett said. "A show bible holds the most important information in a production, so I have a feeling the legendary version must hold some pretty important information."

"Like all the SECRETS of the UNIVERSE?!" Sasha, luckily seat-belted in, exclaimed.

"I mean . . . possibly?" Beckett said. "At this point, I wouldn't be surprised."

"Like where all the missing socks go, and why cats purr,

and whether they named the color orange after the fruit or the fruit after the color!" Sasha was blowing his own mind.

Meanwhile, Reo was in the last row of the van with his headphones on, focused on a deck of tarot cards. He thought about the Show Bible as he shuffled the cards, drew a single card from the top of the deck, and reshuffled, again and again. But something strange was going on. There were seventy-two cards in a tarot deck, so the odds of drawing each individual card is one out of seventy-two. Reo was no mathematician, but it seemed impossible, then, that he was drawing the exact same card, over and over, no matter how he shuffled. He could only stare in amazement as he pulled the Tower. The Tower. The Tower.

CHAPTER 9

WHEN THE VAN FINALLY SLOWED TO A STOP, THE BACKSTAGERS looked out their windows to see a big, rustic brown barn set against the edge of a lush forest.

"Here we are!" Mr. Rample announced, switching off the engine. "The Forest of Arden Theater!"

The boys stepped out of the van and were instantly entranced with the damp smell of leaves, the gentle babble of a nearby stream, and the soft light filtering through the canopy above in golden beams. The Forest of Arden Theater was every bit as magical as the Shakespearean forest it was named for, and this was only the driveway.

"You made it! Ha-HA!" A voice boomed across the serene clearing, making all the Backstagers jump. They turned to see a short woman dressed all in denim with copper skin, a tight and dark fade, and an infectious smile.

"Bert! I want you to meet my boys!" Rample said.

"Ha-HA!" It was unclear what was funny, but she galloped up to where the boys were exiting the van and, despite being total strangers, scooped each of them into a big bear hug.

"I'm Roberta Rodríguez, the production stage manager around here, but if you call me Roberta, I'll have you untangling cords and organizing spike tape all week, just try me! It's Bert, thank you very much!"

"Hey, Bert, I'm Jory! I'm head of wardrobe at Genesius."

"Reo, props."

"I'm Aziz, head carpenter. This place is dope."

"I'm Sasha, head of lighting, and sound, and tool-mouse trainer, and—"

"Beckett. I do a bit of everything, but let's say ASM."

"I'm Hunter, I'm the stage manager. Well, on deck to be, next semester."

"My stage managers! So you guys'll be working with me!" Bert lit up extra-bright. Beckett and Hunter smiled at each other, excited to be acknowledged in their new, advanced roles.

"Should we bring their bags to company housing?" Rample asked.

"Nah, let's leave 'em for now," Bert said. "I wanna get these guys started ASAP. It's load in! We can use all the help we can get!"

THE BACKSTAGERS AND THE FINAL BLACKOUT

Bert led them around the side of the building, away from the big, folksy barn doors to a smaller, gray metal door around back. The stage door. Inside, she gave them each a lanyard with an official Forest of Arden crew badge and led them down a long hallway to a door marked STAGE LEFT.

"Wanna see what we're working with so far?" Bert asked.

"Yes, please!" Sasha cried.

"Ha-HA!" Bert bellowed and swung open the door, letting the guys inside.

"Wow," was all Hunter could say as they stepped out onto the stage and took in the scene.

The big, open auditorium was alive with activity. Drills buzzed, hammers clanged, and a cacophony of voices shouted. A few yards ahead of them, a big drop was being attached to a low-hanging fly rail with the speed and precision of a race-car pit stop before it was hoisted aloft into the fly just moments later. Some of the younger crew people were hauling big tables into the audience, right out over the seats, and setting up computers, controls, and lamps—"For the creative team during tech," Bert informed them. Just past the lip of the stage, an older crew woman, her gray hair tucked into a black baseball cap, climbed into some kind of rolling, walled-in machine that, when wheeled into place, began to lift up impossibly high, to the rail where the lights hung. Once at full height, the gray-haired woman bravely reached out and began adjusting lighting instruments with no fear. Bert informed them that machine was called a Genie, and it was not to be messed with, much to Sasha's disappointment.

A heavily tattooed crew guy trotted up to them. He was dressed in black shorts and a T-shirt, with tall black socks and a newsboy cap.

"Hey, Bert, you want me to set up the calling desk on the deck or in the booth?" he asked.

"Dude, are you brand-new?! Ha-HA! The deck, of course! I wanna be close to the action."

"We call from the deck at our school, too," Hunter said proudly.

"Knew I liked you," Bert said. "Everybody, this is Thom, he's head electrics here."

Thom took off his cap and twirled it in greeting.

"Oh WOW," Sasha said. "I'm head electrics, too!"

"Good to meet ya, my dude!" Thom said, extending a bear-paw hand to warmly shake Sasha's. "You wanna come help me set up the calling desk and monitors? Then I can show you our board. She's brand-new and she's *beautiful*."

"I'd LOVE to!" Sasha said.

"I'll send him your way in a minute," Bert said. "I'm gonna introduce all you guys to the department heads so we can put you to work and get you some big-kid experience! But first, I wanna show you the oldest part of our backstage. Copy?" she asked, a knowing twinkle in her eye.

"Copy," Reo said, resolute.

Bert and Rample led the Backstagers through some tunnels under the stage to the trap room—the room where the automation team piloted the elevators and trap doors. At the very back of this low, cavernous space was a small door labeled just like it was in their Club Room: UNSAFE.

"Of course, Rample told me why you guys are *really* here," Bert whispered as she took a ring of keys from her belt loop. "I do hope you get your backstage problems figured out before the end of the week, though, because we really do want your help on the show!"

She slid an old key into the lock on the door and opened it, revealing a welcome sight: the starry void of the tunnels of the backstage. Hunter breathed a sigh of relief on behalf of everyone.

"Now, you were all careful about keeping your phones off, right?" Rample asked.

The Backstagers all nodded.

"Then we shouldn't have to worry about Thiasos following you here, though I'm sure they're expecting you to find some way into the backstage during your week off."

Just then, a short, wiry crew person approached the crowd of them from behind.

"Hey, Bert," they said. "I doubt we're getting to auto-mation until—oh wow, the door's open!"

"Oh hey, Nik! Everybody, this is Nik. They're head of automation." Nik was scarcely taller than tiny Sasha, so the low ceiling of the trap room wasn't a bother to them at all. They wore a black beanie that concealed all but a few strands of their neon pink hair.

"And yeah," Bert continued, "I'm just giving them the full tour."

"Funny," Nik said, "I've never seen this door open before. There are a bunch of legends about it, though, and with the lock on it and the ominous 'Unsafe' label, I was kind of expecting something more exciting than an empty closet!"

Sasha looked through the open door into the vast, cosmic nothingness of the tunnels and then back to Nik, who looked unimpressed.

"Yeah," Bert replied, "I know, something about a gas leak a long time ago. I keep it locked and labeled just to be safe."

"Huh, I'm gonna keep this revelation to myself, so the legends can live on. Anyway," Nik said with a yawn, "I'm not gonna need to get into any automation stuff until Tuesday at least, so I'm wondering if I might be useful somewhere else."

"Why don't you check in with the puppet designer and see if she's planning to automate any of the plant's movements?"

"Great thinking. Nice to meet y'all!" Nik said, before they left the trap room.

After a quiet moment, Bert let out a "Ha-HA!" Bert had this way of using her guttural belly laugh to mean any number of things. Just now it seemed to mean *the coast is clear.*

"What was that all about?" Jory asked. "Nik couldn't see the tunnels! They thought it was just an empty closet!"

"Most crew folks don't know a thing about the REAL backstage that's past the Unsafe doors of the world," Bert said. "You have to discover it when you're young, before you decide that you know what's possible and impossible. Luckily, you guys found it in time. My crew? They missed out. If they hadn't, I would put tech on hold and have the whole theater helping you guys out. But sadly, they're just regular crew folks. You're Backstagers."

"Why can you see the backstage, then?" Jory asked.

"Because I was taken through the Unsafe door at Penitent Angels when I was your age," Bert replied.

"You're looking at my very own date to Dance at the Gym," Rample said, beaming. "She was the first person I called when I lost my job at Genesius, and luckily she had a spot for me on the crew here."

"Once a Backstager, always a Backstager," Bert said, eyes twinkling.

"So," Rample said. "Any ideas of where to start looking for the Show Bible?"

"I think I have one," Reo replied. "I'll need some thread so I can find my way back in case I get lost. And some solitude. You can all pitch in upstairs with tech. I'll be all right."

"Take a walkie, just in case," Hunter said. "If you run into any trouble, any at all, call and we'll be there in an instant."

The Genesius crew each gave Reo an encouraging hug and dispersed.

Bert brought Reo a long spool of red cord and a walkie. He tied the end of the cord to a pillar in the trap room and carried the spool with him, unraveling it slowly as he walked, creating a tether back to the world outside the backstage. He stepped into the Unsafe door, looked back to Bert, and nodded bravely as she shut the door behind him.

Now Reo stood surrounded by darkness and stars. Unlike the frenzy of the tech upstairs, the tunnels were perfectly silent. Most kids would be scared to be alone in such a place, but Reo learned to trust himself in quiet solitude a long time ago.

He pulled a single tarot card from his pocket. It was the Tower: a foreboding picture of a tall dark stone tower at the moment it's struck by lightning, sending its inhabitants falling helplessly into the depths below. He focused on the image, memorizing every detail. Then, when he could picture the place in his mind with perfect clarity, he closed his eyes, held the spool of cord in front of him, and began to walk.

CHAPTER 10

DRIVING DOWN THE COMMERCIAL STRIP OF MAPLE AVENUE EN route to St. Genesius at what felt like the earliest hour any human had ever been awake in recorded history, a million things ran through Timothy's mind. He needed to know what was up with the guys. He needed to get back into the Club Room and salvage what relics of past shows he could, or else let them be lost forever. He needed COFFEE. The last thing he needed was to take exams all day in subjects that he would never study again once he started school for stage management at Wolverine University.

"Let's just drive past the school," he said to Jamie, who sat in the passenger's seat, uncharacteristically quiet. "Let's just keep driving until we get to the airport, then get on a flight as far away as we can. Somewhere beachy."

"Heh, yeah. That would be nice," Jamie said.

"What's stopping us, honestly? We're already accepted to Wolverine! We're never gonna need quadratic equations or the structure of cells or the details of the Louisiana Purchase or *Latin*. This is all so pointless!"

"Well, there is some financial aid we can apply for with the results," Jamie said. "So I'm focusing on that."

"Ugh, why are you always right?" Timothy said, playfully butting Jamie's shoulder with his head. "I'm just gonna focus on this fall, when we're on our own on that big old campus. Won't it be something to meet up for breakfast in the student union every chilly morning and walk to classes together? Classes in things we *actually* want to study? Heck, I'm even excited to go to football games!"

"Now you're talking crazy," Jamie said with a laugh.

"I'll learn to love them, because I'll be there with you."

Jamie didn't say anything back, but he reached over and grabbed Timothy's hand. They drove in silence for a moment. Then, Jamie saw something unexplainable.

"What in the *world* . . ." he whispered as he pointed to a billboard towering over the busiest intersection on Maple Avenue.

"Whoa," Timothy said.

THE SHOW MUST GO ONWARD!

BLAKE MCQUEEN

FOR ST. GENESIUS DRAMA CLUB PRESIDENT

"I can't believe it," Timothy said. "How much do you think that cost?!"

"Probably a whole semester's tuition," Jamie said, shaking his head. "Some people . . ."

They parked in the student lot and lumbered toward the school, flanked by dozens of other weary-looking seniors. When they reached the front doors, they were stopped by a flyer in their faces.

"Kevin McQueen for Drama Club Presi—oh," Kevin McQueen said. "Sorry, I didn't realize it was you guys."

"No worries," Jamie said. "What are you doing out here? Only the underclassmen in the Drama Club can vote in the election. Why hand out flyers to all of the seniors?"

"We're trying to make the whole school aware of the issues at play here." He gestured to a small folding table with a hand-drawn campaign sign next to the front doors, where a couple of Onstagers were speaking to students and handing out homemade brochures. "I feel like if everyone is talking about this, it might show some of the undecided Onstagers that the majority of the student body stands with you guys."

"I appreciate that," Timothy said, "but maybe you should—"

"Oh!" Kevin interrupted. "Would you wanna man the table for a period or two when you have a break in your exam schedule? I think that hearing directly from the Backstagers would be a really effective way to reach—"

"Kevin, we'd love to," Jamie said, "but don't you think it's going to be hard to make any noise with that billboard out there?"

"What billboard?" Kevin asked. Timothy and Jamie shared a look.

CHAPTER 11

SAAAAAASHAAAAAAA," THE VOICE COOED. "SAAAAASHA. SASHA. Sasha."

Sasha opened his eyes.

He was suspended in an iridescent pink mist, infinitely vast in all directions. Shining bubbles of all sizes slowly rose all around him—or were they falling? It was impossible to tell, because the space had no up or down.

When Sasha's vision cleared, he saw the source of the beautiful voice that called his name: a gentle being made of pure light.

"Genius!" Sasha called. "It's good to see you!"

"It's good to see you, too, Sasha," the muse said. Sasha had not seen his muse since they gifted him the Master Switch, deep in the backstage.

"Where are we?" Sasha asked.

"In your mind. I think it's very lovely here."

"It IS. I've never looked this deeply inside my own mind before."

"Well, it's here for you whenever you need a peaceful space of your own."

"What are we doing here?" Sasha asked. "Is there something you need to tell me?"

"I appear when you have an idea, or rather when you are about to have an idea. I am the herald of epiphany," Genius replied. "So perhaps there is something *you* must tell *me*."

Sasha thought hard for a minute. He'd been turning the Backstagers' dilemma over and over in his head and couldn't think of a way out of it. He did have a lot of questions for Genius, though.

"Can I ask you something instead?"

"Of course," Genius said. "I'm here for you."

"Why me?" Sasha asked. "Why am I the only Backstager with a muse? Why was I chosen for the Master Switch? What is going to happen now that it's lost?"

Genius chuckled softly and said, "Oh, Sasha. I am but a reflection of your own mind. I can't know what's in the future. But let me ask *you* a question now. Why *not* you?"

"Huh?"

"Why shouldn't you be the special one? Because you are

smaller than the others? Because you lead with your heart? Because you make mistakes sometimes? Because you see the world with those wide-open eyes of yours?"

Sasha had never thought about it before, but put like that, he realized that none of those things ought to make someone unworthy of special talents.

"Maybe I am here to remind you not to diminish yourself or your ideas, even if the rest of the world does. When your intuition strikes, *trust it.*" The muse smiled and began to glow even brighter, incandescent like the sun. "Because even if no one else knows, you and I know that your ideas are truly . . ."

"Genius," Sasha whispered, as he snapped awake.

✕

"What?" Jory asked.

He was standing over Sasha's bed. Sasha rubbed his eyes and sat up. It took Sasha a moment to get his bearings. The room was dark but for a tiny nightlight that illuminated the side of Jory's face. The air had the damp smell of spring in the woods and the crickets outside were singing loud enough to make themselves heard over the whirring fan that sat slowly turning beside an open window. Yes, they were still in the company housing at the Forest of Arden. He turned to look at the little digital clock next to his bed. 3:33 a.m.

"Nothing, sorry," Sasha said. "Just a dream."

"Sorry to wake you," Jory said, "but you have to get up and get dressed."

"Is something wrong? Is it Thiasos?"

"Reo's back. And he's found something."

Sasha got dressed quickly, and he and Jory tiptoed down to the common room, where the other Backstagers were gathered around a single lantern and Reo. Beckett brought Reo a cup of tea, and he sipped it slowly, a serious look on his face.

"Reo, are you okay?" Sasha whispered.

"I am, thanks Sasha."

"What did you find?" Aziz asked.

"Give him a minute," Beckett said.

"No, it's okay, we have no time to waste," Reo replied. He set down the cup of tea. "On our way here, I decided to ask my cards for a clue about where to start looking. I kept drawing the same card, again and again—the Tower. I used that image as my focal point and wandered the tunnels. How long has it been?"

"Two days," Hunter replied.

"Wow. Anyway, I just held that image in my mind as I walked and suddenly . . . there it was."

"What?" Jory asked.

"The Tower itself. A huge, stone tower, just like on the card, standing right in the middle of the tunnels. I tied the cord I'd brought to the front door and followed the strand back. It will lead us directly there."

"Reo, that's excellent!" Aziz said, leaping to his feet. "Let's get our supplies together and head there now."

"Wait," Reo said, stopping him. Aziz sat again. "There's something you all have to know about the Tower card in tarot. It's . . . intense."

"Intense how?" Beckett asked.

"It means a final reckoning. A violent upheaval. Permanent change. When the Tower shows up in a reading, you can expect your status quo to be burnt to the ground so that something new can begin."

"So what does it mean for us?" Hunter asked.

"I just have this feeling . . . this intuition . . ."

Sasha's eyes widened a bit.

"I feel like once we walk through the doors of that Tower," Reo said, "nothing will ever be the same. That it's the point of no return."

CHAPTER 12

"RE YOU ALIVE?"

"No."

"But you're an animal?"

"YES."

"So you're dead?"

"Big surprise there."

"Shhh, Dimitri. Okay, so you're a dead animal."

"Don't waste questions, Dia."

"Don't tell me how to play the game, Aleka."

"We're almost there, guys," Niko said. "Okay, do you have fur?"

"Yes," Tasia replied. She chewed the end of her long blond hair like a pacifier.

"Are you big or small?"

"Small."

"Are you a rat?"

"No."

"Strange, you look like a rat." Aleka hissed, pulling her long black hair away from her face as if she were lifting a veil just to hurl the insult.

"That's not FUNNY!" Tasia shouted as she picked up a book off the stack on the floor and tossed it at Aleka. Aleka dodged it, catlike, and furrowed her brow. Just as she was about to pounce, her brother Niko stood and restrained her.

"Okay," Niko said. "Maybe it's time for another game."

But it wasn't the game that was grating on the Thiasos Backstagers. Even if they were sitting in total silence with their eyes shut, they could all feel the walls of the youth wing of Thiasos headquarters closing in on them. It was just big enough to hold beds and trunks for the five of them, so each Backstager made sure their personal space was very clearly theirs. The result was a tiny room that looked like a Frankenstein's monster of five separate rooms smashed together. It was a jumbled, cluttered space and they had been locked there, with all privileges revoked, ever since the fiasco with the God Mic.

Aleka and Niko should have known better than to swipe one of Thiasos's artifacts and go after Jory's Designer's Notebook on their own, but they'd just wanted to make their mom proud. The gamble had landed them here, locked in a small dormitory with a pile of boring Greek mythology books they'd all read a hundred times, a puzzle of the Parthenon, and the company of their fellow Backstagers. That company had grown stagnant after a couple of weeks of confinement, and now they all seemed poised to rip each other to shreds at any moment.

"How about the compliments game?" Niko asked. "I'll go first. Aleka, that particular shade of black you're wearing really suits your—"

"Shut up," Aleka said, in no mood for Niko's signature charm. Niko shrugged his shoulders and went back to admiring his olive complexion and perfectly sleek hair in a mirror on the wall.

"Yes, how about we all just shut up," Dimitri suggested, his already low, droll voice descending to depths that seemed impossible for a human voice to go.

"Thought you'd never ask," Dia said as she scribbled a doodle in marker on the toe of her sneaker. With her multiple piercings, bracelets, chains, and choker, the doodle was just one more embellishment on the walking canvas that was Dia.

The Thiasos Backstagers retreated to their beds.

There was peace for maybe forty-five seconds, until Tasia blurted out, "For the record, I was a dead SQUIRREL."

And in an instant, Aleka was on top of Tasia, bashing her

with her own pillow as hard as she could. Niko and Dimitri leaped up to stop the onslaught while Dia just rolled her eyes and kept doodling. The scuffle was interrupted by a knock at the door before any real damage could be done.

"Lunch already?" Niko wondered as he quickly worked to smooth the hairs that had fallen out of place.

"I say, when they come in here with the food," Tasia said, a mess of frizzy blond tangles and torn frills, "we REVOLT! And ESCAPE!" She marched to the door and shouted to the other side, "I hope you're serving JUSTICE today, because we're serving REVENGE!"

She swung the door open and gasped when she was met not by a Thiasos grunt with a platter of underwhelming lunch but by an immaculately dressed woman with a sweeping white hairstyle and a sly expression.

"MADAM THIASOS," Tasia cried, backing away and lowering her eyes. "Forgive me, I was only playing around."

"Playing is for little girls," Madam Thiasos said. Tasia nodded and retreated back to her bed.

"Mother," Aleka said. "To what do we owe the pleasure?"

"I'm here with good news," Madam Thiasos said, twisting her lips to a shape that would be a smile if there were any kindness in her heart. "My plan has been executed perfectly and is now complete. We have secured the legendary artifacts that Genesius was hiding: our God Mic, the

Master Switch, the Designer's Notebook, and, much to our surprise, the Ghost Light as well."

"They had the Ghost Light, too?" Niko whispered, amazed. "That means—"

"We now have all but one," Madam Thiasos said. "The Show Bible."

"Where do you think it is?" Niko asked.

"If we knew that, *dear*, we'd already have it and would be ready for the Final Blackout, wouldn't we?"

Niko lowered his eyes.

"Naturally the Show Bible might take years, or even generations to find," Madam Thiasos said.

Aleka, who'd been shielding herself behind her dark hair, lifted the veil once again to say, "I know how to find it."

Niko's eyes darted to his sister. They were already in enough trouble.

Madam Thiasos let out a strange expiration, half gasp, half laugh.

"Oh *do* you?" she said. "Because it seems to me, *daughter dear,* that your bold ideas about how to find the artifacts landed you all in here."

"I found them, didn't I?" Aleka said.

"Aleka!" Niko scolded.

"Without me, Thiasos would still be looking for the Switch, the Notebook, and the Ghost Light. I found them in a few weeks when the organization was taking years."

"And lost one of ours in the process!" Madam Thiasos cried.

"So it's clear, then," Aleka said, standing, "that we have to work together."

She and her mother stared each other down for a tense beat as Tasia mouthed "Oh. My. GOSH," to Dimitri across the room.

Finally, Madam Thiasos narrowed her eyes and asked, "*How*, pray tell, do you think you'll find the Show Bible?"

"Let us out of here and I'll show you," Aleka said. "We can start right now if you'd like."

Madam Thiasos smiled. She'd raised her daughter well.

><

Madam, Aleka, Niko, Dimitri, Dia, Tasia, and two burly, suited Thiasos security guards swept across the lawn toward the cliff at the edge of headquarters property in focused silence. They descended the stone staircase down to a platform overlooking the sea where a small cave was carved into the rock. Inside the cave there was a boulder, which the two security guards rolled aside, revealing an ancient carved archway leading to a sea of stars. It was the original entrance to the backstage.

The Thiasos crew stepped into the darkness of the tunnels and Aleka reached into a satchel that hung at her side. She pulled out a small wooden box with a metal sliding control on its face and said, "Master Switch, light our way to the Show Bible."

She slid the control up and a pool of light appeared a few feet ahead of them. Aleka stepped into the light. It began to dim just as another pool appeared a few feet deeper into the tunnels. She proceeded to the next pool, which produced yet another. It was a path.

"Are you coming?" Aleka called back to her mother.

Madam Thiasos nodded to her daughter, impressed.

CHAPTER 13

WHOA," JORY SAID.

"Yeah," was all Hunter could muster.

They stood alongside Beckett, Aziz, Sasha, and Reo looking upward in awe.

They'd followed Reo's red cord through twists and turns of the tunnels for hours until they reached its end. Reo had tied the cord to the handle of a stark iron door at the base of a monumental, ominous tower. Its walls were free of windows, gargoyles, or ornamentation of any kind, though it was topped with a crown-like turret that nearly touched the black storm clouds swirling above it. A flash of lighting struck the crown, illuminating its red and gold paint and making the Backstagers jump.

"We're not actually going *in* there," Beckett said.

"Yeah, there might as well be a sign that says, 'Your grisly death, right this way,'" Aziz said.

"We'll be together," Hunter said, looking to Jory, who nodded back bravely. "We got this."

As they stepped up to the iron door and pulled it open, they all braced for sheer terror and certain doom. They were surprised then when they were met not with a house of horrors but with a gorgeous lobby, straight out of a Jazz Age hotel.

Stepping inside, the Backstagers marveled at the gilded walls, plush sofas of leather and green velvet, painted glass lamps, and gleaming wooden tables that surrounded them. Framed paintings and photographs covered the walls depicting dancing couples in beads and top hats, bottles of champagne mid-pop, and tuxedoed horn players wailing away. Jazz music played softly from a Victrola, the earliest kind of home music system, in the corner. There was a reception desk to their right that was unremarkable, except for the fact that it was unmanned. Directly across from the front door was an ornate elevator.

". . . Not what I was expecting," Reo said.

"Don't you dare sound disappointed," Beckett said, chuckling.

"The Show Bible has got to be on the top floor, right?" Sasha said. "In video games, the loot is ALWAYS on the top floor."

"After a crazy boss battle," Aziz said darkly.

"Well, luckily there's an elevator," Hunter said. "Let's go!"

They pushed the call button for the elevator and its doors whooshed open, revealing a shining brass cage car. They stepped in and saw that instead of buttons for each individual floor there was just one, labeled UP.

"Here goes nothing," Hunter said as he pushed the button.

And nothing is just what they got. Even though the button lit up, the elevator didn't even twitch. He pressed the button again. Nothing.

"It couldn't have been that easy," Jory said.

"Let's take a look around the lobby," Hunter said. "Maybe there's a hidden staircase or something."

They exited the car and began to scour the room. Beckett made his way over to the reception desk, where he found a typewritten note.

"You guys," he called. "You'd better get a look at this!"

The Backstagers gathered around as Beckett read the message.

```
YOU CAME TO SEEK AN ANCIENT TOME
BUT IF YOU PLAN TO TAKE IT HOME
AND GAIN THE KNOWLEDGE IN ITS PAGES,
PROVE YOUR OWN, UPON THESE STAGES
```

"Oh COOL," Sasha said. "It's like that movie with the kids looking for the pirate treasure!"

"Except this isn't a movie, Sash," Aziz said.

"So . . . we have to prove our own knowledge," Hunter said.

"The test has already started," Reo said. "We're in a trial right now."

"We have to make the elevator go," Hunter said, "and it will take our own knowledge to solve!"

"Maybe it's an electrical problem?" Beckett said. "I'll look for the fuse box!" He walked over to one of the walls and began to inspect each painting and photograph for a hidden compartment.

"I'll help!" Sasha said. He searched the opposite wall.

"Maybe there is some clue back here," Reo said as he made his way behind the reception desk. The wall was covered in hanging rings of keys and he jiggled each, hoping to find some kind of switch.

"I'm gonna take another look at the elevator," Hunter said. "Maybe there is something we missed."

"Copy," Aziz said. "I'm wondering if we're thinking about this wrong. Maybe the elevator is a red herring and we're actually supposed to *descend* to find the Show Bible. That would be some pretty sick design. Maybe there's a trap door?" He started stomping around the red carpet, listening for the hollow sound of a hidden door.

"Good thinking!" Hunter called back as he pored over each nook and cranny of the elevator cage for clues.

Meanwhile, Jory was searching the poem itself, turning over each word in his mind.

Prove your own, upon these STAGES, he thought. *Why would they call them stages? And who is they?*

He sat on one of the velvet couches, just a few feet from the scratchy Victrola, and after a while he couldn't help but tap his foot to the tune absentmindedly.

"Everything dah dah totally current . . ." he sang along softly. "Dah dah dah dah . . ."

He leaped up from his seat.

"WAIT! GUYS! I know this song!"

"That's great, Jor," Beckett called back as he and Sasha worked together to try to wrestle a huge painting of a flapper girl off the wall. "Maybe you can sing it to us, while you lend a hand?!"

"This song . . . this lobby . . . the poem." Jory's mind was racing. Hunter took notice and emerged from the elevator.

"What's the matter, Jory?"

"The poem said to prove our knowledge upon these stages. We're not in a *lobby*, we're on a stage! This is a set!"

The others stopped what they were doing and looked around.

"The set of what?" Aziz asked.

"This jazz song is from a musical!" Jory said. "My mom used to play the cast album in the car. It's the title song from *Totally Current Billy!*"

"Oh YEAH!" Sasha said. "I remember that from the Tonys!"

"It's all about flappers in a Jazz Age hotel!" Jory said. "This is the hotel lobby set from the show!"

"Great work, Jory!" Hunter threw a beefy arm around his wiry boyfriend affectionately.

"Is there anything special about the elevator in the show?!" Aziz asked.

"Oh my gosh, YES! I know how to—" Jory said, before his face fell. "Oh . . ."

"What is it?" Reo asked.

"Well," Jory said, "in the musical, the hotel elevator is a special model that is powered by . . . tap dancing."

"Oh," Aziz said. "Oh crap."

"Yeah," Jory said. "So I really don't know how to solve that."

"No, no, there has to be a way," Hunter said.

"Can you enchant our feet, Reo?" Sasha asked.

"Dude, I'm a witch, not Gandalf," Reo replied.

"Well then, what now?" Hunter said. "We're so close!"

"Maybe I can construct some kind of device to simulate the taps," Aziz offered.

Throughout all this, Beckett's head sunk so low, it seemed likely to fall off of his shoulders and roll out the front door. He took a deep breath and sulked his way over to the elevator. Once inside, he rubbed his face, straightened his body, and began to shuffle his feet.

The guys stopped talking as they noticed Beckett performing a perfectly respectable time step. The elevator slowly began to rise.

"Beckett!" Jory said. "You're doing it!"

Beckett stopped the dance and the elevator sunk back down to the lobby level again.

"I was forced to take lessons as a kid," Beckett said sternly, "and we are NEVER going to speak of this, ever again."

"Deal," Reo said.

"Yeah I can handle that," Hunter said.

"Beckett, you can DANCE!" Sasha said before Aziz clapped a hand over his mouth.

"Shall we?" Reo asked.

The Backstagers entered the elevator once again, and when they were all ready, Beckett began to tap. Jory took Hunter's hand as they all rose toward the next challenge.

CHAPTER 14

"TWO DAYS," BAILEY GROANED. "COME ON, NO ONE IS OUT OF cell service for two whole days."

Adrienne looked to Chloe, who looked at the carpet. They were sitting cross-legged on either side of Bailey on her bed, offering what support they could. Chloe had rejoined the Penitent Backstagers earlier that winter, and Adrienne had caught her up on Thiasos and the artifacts. Now, they both wished they were as clueless about it all as Bailey so that they might console their friend without lying to her at the same time.

What were they supposed to say? Tell Bailey not to worry because Beckett was actually in a magical parallel dimension trying to save the world, and in that dimension, time functions differently, so he probably didn't realize he'd left her on the hook for two whole days? Yeah, no.

"They're in *tech*," Chloe stressed. "You know how the-ater kids lose all sense of time during tech." It wasn't a lie, exactly, though Chloe's delivery of the line was about as natural as her dyed silver hair.

"Not Beck," Bailey said. "Having a schedule is the only thing that grounds his energy. If he loses track of time, he gets anxious."

"But this isn't a school show," Adrienne said, "this is professional. Who knows how hard they are working him over at Forest of Arden."

"I kissed him," Bailey blurted out.

Adrienne took her hand.

"What?" Chloe said.

"At the Dance at the Gym. I thought we were ready, but ever since that night he has been *so weird*. We've barely talked, and he keeps making excuses to get off the phone with me and . . . even that night! We were all set to get burgers at Hand Jive and then all of a sudden everyone has food poisoning? I mean, come *ON*, that's obviously fake. Adrienne, you were there with them in the Club Room . . ."

Adrienne turned as pink as her hair.

"I don't mean to put you on the spot," Bailey said, "but please, can you just tell me what actually happened? I won't tell Beckett you told me, I promise. I just have to know I didn't, like, screw anything up."

Adrienne didn't know what to say. She stammered for a moment before Chloe said, "Okay, enough is enough."

Bailey turned to Chloe, whose eyes shimmered with tears. This had been a long time coming.

"I can't lie to you," Chloe said. "Gosh, after the whole *Phantasm* thing, I already owe you enough explanations and apologies—but that's for another time."

Bailey was confused. "Chloe, what are you—"

"There's something we need to tell you . . . but I think it's going to be easier if we show you. Don't you think so, Adrienne?"

Adrienne let out a deep sigh, because she could feel it, just like Chloe: Now was the time.

"Yeah," she said. "I think you're right."

"You guys are freaking me out," Bailey said. "I'm gonna need some answers here."

"Tomorrow," Chloe said. "While the senior girls are taking their exams, meet us in the auditorium."

"The auditorium?"

Adrienne nodded. "There's more to the backstage than you know about."

CHAPTER 15

WHEN THE ELEVATOR SLOWED TO A HALT AND THE DOORS SLID open with a *ding*, the Backstagers finally understood just how much magic was contained in this tower. Having first dealt with a very ordinary and contained lobby, they were shocked to now be met by a clearing in a dark, dense forest on the night of a giant full moon. The air was fresh and cool like that first night of autumn and dank with the aroma of wood, soil, and pine.

Hunter swallowed hard, and said, "Well, I guess we're here."

He led his crew out of the elevator, and when the doors shut behind them, the elevator vanished completely. Now there was no evidence that they were in a tower at all. The night sky hung as high over their heads as the sky in the real world, and the sounds of the forest were just as mysterious.

Reo pulled his dark cloak a little tighter around himself and looked up at the giant silver-blue harvest moon.

"At least she's here," he said, bowing his head to it reverently.

"Let's look around this clearing," Hunter said. "Maybe there's, like, a map, or some instruction." The guys nodded and began to walk around the open clearing.

"So what show do we think this is?" Jory asked.

"Um, forest shows . . ." Beckett scanned his brain like a search engine scouring data. "Could be that medieval show *Castlelot*?"

"Ohhh maybe!" Sasha said. "Or that Shakespeare one? I don't speak Shakespeare, but I remember there were fairies and a magical forest and someone turned into a donkey and—WHOA!"

Sasha suddenly found himself facedown in a ditch.

"Careful!" Aziz said, rushing over to help his friend up. When he got over to the ditch, though, he froze.

Hunter kicked some dirt in frustration and called into the night, "Okay! If you're gonna give us a test, we at least need a clue or something!"

Jory locked eyes with Aziz and said, "Uh . . . Hunter?"

"Like, can we even know what show we're in?!" Hunter shouted. Now Reo and Beckett were staring at Sasha as he dusted himself off. Jory moved toward Hunter slowly.

"Hunter," he whispered, "maybe shouting isn't—"

"What are you waiting for?!" Hunter cried toward the moon. "WHAT ARE YOU—"

Jory clasped his hand over Hunter's mouth. Hunter looked to him, confused, and Jory pointed to the ditch that Sasha had stumbled into. Hunter's eyes widened because he finally noticed that it wasn't a ditch at all. It was a footprint. A giant-sized footprint.

"Wh-what . . ." Beckett stammered, "is THAT?"

"I know what show we're in," Hunter whispered. "Genesius did it my first semester as a Backstager."

The sound of distant thunder echoed through the wood.

"It's *Forest for the Trees,* the fairy-tale musical."

"What's it about?" Sasha asked, as Aziz lifted him out of the footprint.

"It's, like, this mash-up of all these different fairy tales," Hunter said as the sound of thunder intensified. Reo looked up suspiciously at the cloudless night sky again.

"And the characters band together to defeat a rampaging—"

"GIANT!" Sasha screamed as he pointed upward to the canopy of trees.

The moon hanging above them was suddenly eclipsed by a massive head and shoulders above the tree line. Several stories tall, the giant's rosy pink face twisted into a snarl as he let out an angry roar. He wore rustic burlap pants held up by suspenders of thick rope. His untamed red hair and flowing red beard caught the wind and flew about his furious face as if he had a halo of pure flame.

"Run for it!" Hunter shouted.

The Backstagers took off in a sprint, slipping into the dark cover of the trees and staying low as they raced away from the clearing.

"Where are we going?!" Sasha called before Aziz shushed him and whispered, "We don't know, Sash, just RUN!"

The giant spanned the clearing in just a few paces and hit the tree line, wading through hundreds-of-years-old oaks and pines as if they were bothersome weeds. The Backstagers were able to keep a safe distance between them and the rampaging beast, though they had no idea where they were going.

They crested a hill and looked around, trying to decide which way to go.

"Are we supposed to beat this thing?!" Beckett said.

"Your guess is as good as mine," Hunter said.

"Well we can't just run forever," Jory said.

"Do we have another option?" Reo asked.

"How about we hide?!" Sasha suggested as he pointed to a tiny brick cottage a few paces away, hidden among the trees.

"Makes sense to me!" Hunter said.

"Wait, how do we know there isn't something more terrifying living in there?" Aziz asked. But when he heard the crashing of trees and the roars of the giant growing closer, he said, "Oh, whatever. Let's hurry!" and they dashed up to the cottage's front door.

Aziz jiggled the handle, but the door didn't budge. "Locked!"

"Force it!" Hunter commanded, and mercifully, with the weight of six Backstagers against it, the door came loose and all six of them fit safely inside. They slammed the door shut behind them.

Ducking low against one of its windowsills, they watched, barely breathing, as the giant crested the hill and looked around for them, enraged. He began to sniff the air, turning his nose in the direction of the cottage.

"Crap," Beckett whispered.

But then a twig snapped somewhere in the distance and the giant turned his attention toward the sound like a predatory animal. He lumbered off in its direction, and soon, his thunderous stomps faded and the Backstagers exhaled at last.

"I think we're safe," Hunter said.

"What is this place?" Aziz asked as he turned to look around the cottage.

THE BACKSTAGERS AND THE FINAL BLACKOUT

The firelight coming from the small stove in the corner revealed simple furnishings, a wooden cellar door dug into the dirt floor, and thankfully, no apparent monsters.

"Now what?" Reo asked.

"Hunter, what else do you remember about *Forest for the Trees*?" Jory asked.

"The giant is furious because a couple of children stole all the candy from his kingdom," Hunter said.

"So . . . we have to find candy?" Aziz said.

"I have half a candy bar in my back pocket!" Sasha said. "It's . . . like, butt temperature . . ."

"No, in the musical the kids eat it all, so the fairy-tale creatures have to come up with another plan."

"Do you guys hear that?" Beckett asked.

Everyone went quiet, and indeed, there was a strange sound echoing from the cellar door. A low sawing sound underneath higher-pitched squeals and hisses.

"Cool, cool, cool," Aziz whispered, "*monsters.*"

"No, wait," Hunter said. "I remember this scene. The cottage scene took us forever to tech because the actors kept messing up the timing of 'The Blaming Song.'"

"The what?" Reo said.

"Come on," Hunter said. "I have a hunch."

As Hunter lifted the cellar door, light spilled into the cabin and the sawing noise grew louder, echoing against the brick walls until it was almost unbearable. As their ears adjusted, though, the squeals and hisses became clearer, and soon they could make them out as voices.

". . . but if you had offered the kids some of your candy instead of being such a pig—"

"Oh come on, Puss, it was my snack after building all day! Have you ever built a whole house?"

"Leave my brother out of this! You told him where the giant kingdom was!"

"I wanted to know what it's like! Curiosity is in my nature! I'm a cat after all . . ."

The Backstagers descended a flight of wooden steps which led to a dank, earthy cellar. There was a small lantern in the center of the floor, around which three disheveled-looking pigs stood on their hindquarters arguing with a cat wearing very fancy boots and two very plump children in matching Bavarian lederhosen. In the corner, a beautiful girl in a white flowing dress with blond hair and a golden crown was out cold, snoring as loud as a buzz saw.

"But I left the boy and his sister with a babysitter!" the cat argued, gesturing to the sleeping beauty with his tail. "It's not my fault she's so prone to nodding off!"

"So it's her fault?" the youngest pig asked.

"Don't be stupid, brother," the oldest pig scolded. "Why

aren't we blaming the children who STOLE AND ATE THE CANDY IN THE FIRST PLACE?!"

"Once again, my name is Hansel and I am *having* a *growth spurt*, thank you!" the little boy said, crossing his arms. "I live in these woods alone with my sister, Gretel. What are we to eat if not candy?"

"Um, greens?" the cat suggested.

"Well that's just offensive," Gretel said.

"Uh, guys," the middle pig said, gesturing to the Backstagers, who stood slack-jawed on the stairs. Hunter stepped forward and began to speak but was quickly interrupted.

"Great," the oldest pig said, throwing his hooves in the air dramatically. "Now we have to share this hiding spot with even more children!"

"I told you pigs to barricade the door!" Gretel said.

"Nice," the middle pig said, putting a hoof around his younger brother. "Asking us to do even more labor after you *know* our other two houses were blown down by that wolf just days ago. Really *NICE*!"

"Will everyone please KEEP IT DOWN?!" the princess moaned from the corner, not bothering to open her eyes.

The fairy-tale creatures erupted into a shouting match as Hunter turned to his crew.

"We have to get them to stop arguing," Hunter said. "In

the show, they can only defeat the giant when they learn to work together."

"So how do they resolve it?" Jory asked. Hunter furrowed his brow, thinking hard.

"I . . . I can't remember," he said. "It was around this time I had to go back to the dressing room to help a character with a quick change. I never could quite hear this section."

The Backstagers looked to one another, stumped.

"Yeah," Hunter continued. "The actress from Penitent couldn't get the costume on herself because there was a whole transformation effect. She was playing, like . . . some kind of . . . Oh! I remember! I had to help the girl who was playing the Witch get into her transformation costume!"

"Okay?" Aziz said, eager as ever to get to the point.

"She entered at the end of the scene and threatened the characters with a terrible curse if they didn't help her defeat the giant!"

"Oh no," Sasha said. "So you're saying we have to go out there again and find the witch?"

"Not if we brought our own . . ." Beckett said.

All eyes turned to Reo, who looked behind himself before he realized what they were suggesting.

"You *can't* be serious," Reo said.

"Why not?" Jory said.

"Because I'm not that kind of witch," Reo said. "I don't know the first thing about cursing. This isn't, like, a storybook—this is real life!"

Hunter sighed. "It's okay, Reo, you've done your share already. Just . . . let me think . . ."

He sat on the stairs, defeated. He had been able to lead his guys out of so many rough spots before, and now he was being foiled by some arguing fables? Really? Some stage manager he'd make.

But then he realized something. Out of all of the skills a stage manager needed to possess, diffusing tension among a crew was the most important. He didn't need a witch to threaten them with a curse. He needed to be the stage manager he knew he could be. He stood and strode into the middle of the room.

"All right, we need QUIET! IN! THE! HOUSE!" he bellowed in his most authoritative voice.

The three pigs, two cherubic children, and one fashionable cat all fell silent and turned to Hunter, shocked.

"Dang," Aziz whispered, impressed.

Even the princess regained consciousness and groggily sat upright.

Hunter paced around the crowd of fairy-tale creatures.

"This is the sorriest excuse for a crew I've ever seen," he said. "Not because you don't have what it takes to beat that giant but because you can't work together! I mean, come on, we have three master carpenters here."

He gestured to the pigs, who looked at each other and then reluctantly smiled.

"We have a world-class costumer. Puss, those boots are just gorgeous."

Puss looked down at his admittedly stunning footwear and looked back at Hunter, touched.

"Hansel, Gretel. You might think you're just a couple of kids, but if you can follow a trail of candy into a giant's lair, I know you can follow a plan and execute it. That's a valuable skill."

Hansel let out a small belch before looking to his sister, who nodded.

"And then there's this beauty over here in the corner. She might seem like she's slacking on the job, but look at how she can drift off in even the most stressful of circumstances. We can all learn from her. Even though we have to fight a giant, we'll never get anywhere if we don't keep our cool and clear our minds."

The princess's eyes opened a bit wider than before, as if she'd had a sudden jolt of caffeine.

The Backstagers smiled as they watched Hunter be the leader they knew best.

"You might not believe in yourselves right now," he said,

looking to Jory as he repeated his words from the Genesius parking lot. "That's fine. I'll believe in you, if you'll believe in me. Because we're a crew."

Jory smiled proudly.

Hunter smiled back and then wound up for his big finish. "So, what do you say, creatures of the forest? Are we a crew?"

The oldest pig stepped up and put his hoof forward.

"I'm in," he said.

"And me," said his youngest brother.

"Let's go," said the middle.

Puss licked his paw before extending it.

Hansel and Gretel both exclaimed in their native German, "Ja!"

The princess covered a wide yawn with one hand but gave a thumbs-up with the other.

"Well, all right," Hunter said. "I want you to meet my own crew, the Backstagers."

He gestured back to where his friends were gathered, and they waved.

"Together," Hunter said, "we're gonna beat this giant."

✕

Later that night, the giant stirred in his sleep as a pebble nailed him straight on the nose.

Then another.

Then a third.

The giant snapped his eyes open and rose from his resting place in the moonlit clearing, enraged. He blinked his eyes into focus and saw a short, plump little boy in play clothes standing at his massive feet, holding a slingshot.

"I'm the boy you've been looking for!" he called.

The giant growled and raised his foot to stomp the boy flat when another voice called from behind, "No, it is I!"

The giant swung around to see another Hansel standing defiantly across the clearing. This Hansel had longer hair, which was pinned up to look short, but from the giant's height, they looked identical. The giant grunted in confusion.

"Liar, I am the boy!"

"No, me!"

"No, ME!"

A third, then a fourth, then a fifth Hansel popped out from behind trees at the clearing's edge. Their voices sounded more like the squeal of an animal than the holler of a little boy, but they looked absolutely identical to the others, save for slightly flatter, pinker noses.

The giant was charging toward the three pinker Hansels when there was a commotion from the canopy above.

"We are the boy!" cried six young voices in unison as six Hansels dropped from the trees. Now, the giant was surrounded by Hansels and absolutely stupefied.

From a high branch in a nearby tree, the drowsy princess and the cat in boots watched, riveted.

"With your costumes and my makeup, they all look just like Hansel!" the princess said.

"Yes, they look just perfect!" the cat purred.

Down in the clearing, the giant spun around and swiped at the air as the Hansels taunted and dodged him. He shut his eyes and roared into the night, his simple giant's brain overwhelmed.

Up in the tree, the cat carefully removed his stylish leather boots.

"I'm going to make my move!" he said, turning to the princess. But she was down for the count, so he just said, "Whatever," and scampered down the tree.

The cat dashed through the crowd of Hansels, scurrying up the giant's leg and around to the back of his pants. The giant roared and reached for him, but the cat was too fast to catch.

"Now!" cried a particularly tall and solid Hansel with a generous swoop of brown hair.

The cat leaped onto the giant's rope suspenders and gnawed with all his might. One suspender severed and fell. Then the other.

The giant looked down at his burlap pants as they fell, revealing his giant polka-dot boxer shorts. The Hansels all burst out laughing. The giant turned bright red and took off running toward the woods, but the burlap pants caught around his ankles.

"RUN!" the tallest Hansel ordered to the others, and they scattered as the humiliated giant teetered and fell with a loud crash into the trees.

The cat scampered up the giant and examined him before shouting to the Hansels, "He's out cold! The woods are saved!"

The crowd of Hansels cheered. The princess blinked awake and, seeing the hulking giant lying motionless on the ground, joined in.

Six of the Hansels removed their costumes and wiped their faces clean of their rosy-cheeked makeup, revealing themselves to be the Backstagers.

"Boss, defeated! Level UP!" Sasha exclaimed, high-fiving Aziz.

"That was magic," Reo said, shaking his head in disbelief.

Hunter scooped Jory up into a hug and said, "Great work, team!"

"Great thinking, Hunter," Beckett said. "Most definitely stage manager material."

The three pigs, the cat in boots, Hansel and Gretel, and the princess rushed up to them. They all exchanged hugs and congratulations.

"Thank you, Backstagers," the oldest pig said. "We of the woods are forever grateful."

"Now, when you're ready, step into the elevator," the princess said.

The sharp sound of a bell dinged through the trees, and from thin air, elevator doors whooshed open. The Backstagers gazed into its warm light as the princess smiled, wide-awake.

"Your next challenge awaits."

CHAPTER 16

PENCILS DOWN!" MR. GILLILAND ANNOUNCED. "TURN YOUR papers over!"

Jamie dropped his pencil on the desk and collapsed over it as if he'd just crossed the finish line of a triathlon. Timothy reached up from where he sat at the desk behind him and squeezed Jamie's shoulder as if to say, "We did it!"

Timothy knew that Jamie had been dreading the math final the most. Jamie had never been great with numbers. He was more suited to intuitive problem-solving, while math came as easily to Timothy as a dancer counting five, six, seven, eight. It's why they were such a good match, onstage and off.

It was their last exam of the day, but while the rest of the seniors were now free to spend the rest of the day playing

Gamestation or eating junk food or sleeping, Timothy and Jamie finally had the time and energy to worry about the Backstagers.

"Rample says they've been in there for four days now with no contact," Jamie said. "That seems bad."

"Or maybe it's good. Maybe it means they're onto something," Timothy said. "Or maybe it doesn't mean anything, because time has decided to go crazy in the backstage and they think they've only been in there for five minutes."

"Yeah," Jamie said. "Still, I can't help but worry."

"I know," Timothy said as he put his arm around his boyfriend.

They made their way to the student lot where Timothy's car was parked. When they slumped into their seats and Jamie fastened his belt, Timothy didn't turn the key in the engine. Instead, he looked at Jamie affectionately.

"I have something for you," he said. He reached across Jamie to the glovebox, which he opened to reveal a small gift-wrapped box.

"What's this for?" Jamie asked as he took the present, suddenly nervous. "It's not our anniversary, right?"

"I just wanted to be able to make you smile today," Timothy said. "I know how nervous you were for this one. I've actually noticed how anxious you've been all week. But now, no matter what, the exams are behind us and we can just look forward . . . to the future."

Jamie opened the present. It was a knit Wolverine University ski cap, with a pom-pom on the top in the school's signature colors. Jamie teared up. But then the tears started to roll, and after a moment, he was sobbing into the hat.

"Do you . . . love it? Hate it?" Timothy patted his back, but Jamie couldn't stop, so Timothy just leaned over and held him until he could get his breath again.

Finally, Jamie wiped his eyes and said, "It isn't the exam. Well, not exactly."

"Then what is it?" Timothy asked.

"I was nervous about the exams, because I was hoping if I did well, I might be able to apply for some merit scholarships, but I've been talking with my family and even if we had major help . . . they just can't afford to send me to Wolverine University."

Timothy looked at the crumpled hat in Jamie's hands and felt terrible.

"Well, maybe . . ." he said. "Maybe you can just do community this year and rack up some credits and transfer in later."

"I seriously doubt our financial situation will change in a year or so, Tim."

"Yeah, that's—I'm so sorry, Jamie. I hadn't even thought about it."

"I'm just so disappointed. To actually *get in* and not be able to go." He ran his fingers over the yellow and blue "W" embroidered on the now soggy hat. "But most of all, I'm so afraid we'll grow apart."

Timothy looked Jamie right in the eye and said, "Jamie, that isn't going to happen. Even if we have to be apart, I'm not going away."

"That's easy to say now," Jamie whispered. "Sorry. I

mean, thank you for saying that. I just know how this goes. Do you talk to any of the Backstagers who graduated before us anymore?"

Timothy realized that he truly didn't. Before Sasha and Aziz and Hunter and Beckett and Jory and Reo, there had been other Backstagers who showed them the wonder and danger and magic of the backstage. They'd spent countless hours together being stupid in the Club Room or doing wonders during tech. They'd all sworn they'd be best friends forever. But then, each Backstager had graduated and gone off to a school where he'd met a new crew to have new adventures with, and now Timothy and Jamie were lucky to get a few direct messages a year saying hey, or happy birthday, or remember this.

They were both sitting silently with this awful realization when there was a knock on the driver's-side window. They looked up to see Bailey Brentwood standing next to the car with her hands on her hips and her brow furrowed.

Timothy rolled down the window. "Bailey! How are you? What are you doing here?"

"Never mind how I am," Bailey said curtly. "I need your car."

"What?"

Adrienne and Chloe caught up with Bailey, panting.

"Please, Bailey," Chloe said. "Let's just take a minute to talk about this."

"We know it's a lot to take in," Adrienne said.

But Bailey didn't look back at them. She just held her eyes on Timothy as if trying to make him bend to her will with mind control.

"We're going for a ride," she said. "I hope you're done with your exams for the day, because it isn't a short drive to Forest of Arden."

"Um," Timothy said, looking over Bailey's shoulder to the helpless Adrienne and Chloe, "can I just have a quick explanation of—"

"Oh I think it's you Backstagers who owe me an explanation," Bailey said. "Quite a few explanations, actually."

Timothy looked at Jamie, whose eyes said, *Dude, she knows.*

CHAPTER 17

"OH. AWESOME," BECKETT SAID WHEN THE ELEVATOR DOORS DINGED OPEN on the next floor of the tower, though he definitely wasn't feeling awesome about where the Backstagers now found themselves.

It was an abyss of darkness lit only by a single torch that burned atop a simple metal stand a few yards into the space. The torch cast a circle of light onto the rocky ground, but otherwise, the space was absolutely pitch-black.

"There aren't any horror musicals, are there?" Reo asked as they stepped toward the torch.

"Only a couple," Jory said, "but the reviews were scarier than the shows themselves."

They stepped into the darkness and the elevator doors closed behind them and disappeared.

"I guess we're supposed to take this?" Aziz grabbed the

torch from its stand and held it aloft. He walked a few paces and its light bounced off of uneven stone walls. Crystals growing from the stone glittered in the flame.

"We're in a cave, I think," Aziz said.

"Must be a tall one," Beckett said. "I can't see the ceiling."

"Is there a path?" Hunter asked.

Aziz followed the wall around the chamber they were in. It curved in a circular shape just a few yards across and appeared to be totally contained, but then he discovered a narrow passageway leading deeper into the dark.

"This way!" he called, and the Backstagers followed behind him as they explored the narrow tunnel.

Sasha, at the back of the pack, looked up suspiciously.

"Do you guys hear that?" he asked.

"Hear what?" Hunter said.

"I don't know, something up high. Like a . . . fluttering?"

"It's probably the sound of the flame echoing off the walls," Hunter said.

"Let's hope," Beckett said.

They walked on until the passage let out into another cavern. The space around them felt cooler and vaster, even though the Backstagers could see only what their torch illuminated.

"Hey, look at the walls in here," Jory said.

Aziz led the group closer to the wall, and as the torch-light grew, they could more clearly see that in this cavern, the rough walls had been carved and polished into something more like the stone walls of a primitive castle. Aziz lifted the torch higher, and its light revealed writing in ancient, indecipherable glyphs carved right into the walls.

"Could be magical sigils?" Reo said as he marveled at the writing.

"Guys, I see something out in the floor," Hunter said, pointing into the darkness. The others strained their eyes. "Aziz, light our way."

Together, they walked toward the center of the cavern, where they found a large iron basin.

As they surrounded the basin, Beckett ran his fingers along the inside of the bowl and held them up to the group covered in black soot.

"This is for burning things," he said.

"I wonder . . ." Aziz said as he looked at the torch in his hand. He shrugged and tossed it into the basin, which erupted instantly into a roaring bonfire. The Backstagers leaped backward from the flame that illuminated the walls around them.

The room was cylindrical with no other tunnels branching off from it. The bonfire lit the entire perimeter of the chamber, but even its bright light couldn't illuminate the ceiling. The chamber just seemed to reach upward forever into darkness. The strange writing wrapped around the space, all leading to a central mural of some great winged creature.

"Uh-oh," Sasha said.

Suddenly, a row of torches dotting the perimeter of the chamber flicked on several stories above their heads. Then another the same distance above those. Then another, lighting the tall chamber, floor by floor, until finally, the Backstagers could see the domed ceiling of the room hundreds of feet above them. It was dark and textured, as if it were covered in deep black velvet.

"What in the world?" Beckett began to say, before Sasha let out a piercing scream.

The ceiling had eyes. First one pair, glowing yellow against the murky darkness of the dome, then several more, then hundreds, all looking down at the Backstagers.

That's when the first creature descended, dripping away from the dome like a thick drop of oil. It fell for a moment before it extended two leathery wings and began to fly around the space, the torchlight revealing its pointed ears and turned-up snout. One by one, these winged things took to the air until the tall chamber was a cacophony of flapping wings and high-pitched screeches. Then, a jazzy tune began to play.

"Oh my gosh, I know this one." Aziz groaned. "It was the one show my family saw when we went to New York when I was a kid. We're in that dance show, *BATS*."

"What's it about?" Sasha asked, gazing upward in wonder.

"It's about . . . frickin' bats. Whoa!"

One of the twirling, human-sized bats swooped down and grabbed Aziz by the shoulders with two taloned feet. With a thrust of its wings, it soared upward toward the domed ceiling with Aziz in tow.

"Aziz!" Sasha cried.

But they weren't separated for long, because a moment later, another bat dove, grabbed Sasha by the shoulders, and took flight.

Hunter looked to Jory, Beckett, and Reo. Without needing to say a word, they all made a break for it, sprinting back toward the rocky passageway they entered from, but they made it only a few strides before they too were picked up and taken aloft.

As Aziz was carried higher and higher in the chamber, he tried to look down to make sure his friends were okay, but looking to the ground hundreds of feet below him made his stomach turn.

"Please don't hurt us!" he cried in terror. He was surprised when his winged captor spoke back.

"We would never hurt you!" the bat said in a strange, nasally voice. "In fact, we are presenting you with a great honor! An audience with the ancient one!"

"With the . . . what?!"

"Tonight is the night we might reach the great beyond! You've come on a most celestial, angelical night!"

Looking to the top of the chamber, Aziz saw that one very large bat still hung upside down from the dome in a deep slumber. He also saw that there was a ledge just below the dome, about the size of a small stage. The bat flew up to the ledge and hovered over it a moment before dropping Aziz.

It took Aziz a moment to get to his feet, but he was relieved that the platform felt solid, even though he was still a dizzying distance from the stone floor below. Soon, bats carrying Sasha, Jory, Hunter, Beckett, and Reo rose up around him and dropped their cargo safely on the platform.

Sasha practically leaped into Aziz's embrace as the others dusted themselves off and caught their breath.

"Everyone okay?" Aziz asked.

Beckett looked at Aziz quizzically and announced, "I am so very, very far from okay."

"What do we think the task is?" Jory asked.

"My bat spoke to me," Aziz said. "It said we're here to meet the . . . ancient one?"

"I am not an 'it,'" squealed a voice. The Backstagers turned to see Aziz's bat flitting around the platform gracefully. "I am Stinklebruiser, the Aromatic Bat!"

"And I am FlippyFlappySpots, the Dandy Bat!" called another, mid–barrel roll.

"I am Charcuterie, the Culinary Bat!"

"Mysterygloves, the Enigmatic Bat!"

"I hate this show," Aziz whispered.

"I heard that," Stinklebruiser said. "Celestial bats are very good hearers!"

"What's a celestial bat?" Sasha asked.

"DON'T answer that," Aziz cried. "It's like, a whole thing. We'll be here all night."

"Who is the ancient one?" Jory asked.

"I am," rumbled a voice. The full chamber of diving and spinning bats gasped in unison, which was a sound so high-pitched and piercing, the Backstagers grabbed their ears to dampen it. The bats all took perches around the walls of the chamber, and the room became suddenly still.

The lone bat hanging from the dome opened his glowing eyes at last and spread his wings, displaying an imposing wingspan of several yards. He was larger than the other bats and grayer, too, with a few holes in the leathery skin of his wings and a bite taken out of his right ear. This bat had seen some things.

"Welcome, Backstagers," he said in an impossibly deep voice.

"You know who we are," Reo said.

"I know everything," the bat replied. "I am Old Chiroptera, the ancient one. Ruler of the Kingdom of Night, and Guardian of the Doors to the Great Beyond."

"Nice to meet you, Citronella!" Sasha called, before he was quietly shushed by Aziz.

"On this night," Chiroptera said, "the night of the Black Wing Moon, any bat who can impress me sufficiently will be granted entry to the Great Beyond. Fail, and you must wait for the next Black Wing Moon, one hundred years from now."

"Get all that?" Beckett said.

"It made even less sense onstage," Aziz replied. "One moment, Your Celestialness."

He turned in to the group of Backstagers and huddled them up.

"This is the task," he said. "We have to impress the old guy and then we'll ascend to the next level."

"How do we impress him?" Hunter asked.

"Good question," Aziz said. "In the show, they just, like, did a talent show."

"YES!" Old Chiroptera bellowed. "A show of your talents!"

"I keep forgetting they have, like, supersonic hearing," Aziz said. "So . . . who's first?"

The Backstagers looked at each other wide-eyed. Their talents were designed to be invisible. After all, they were the ones who made magic behind the scenes.

"I can roll my tongue?" Beckett offered meekly.

"I can say hello in, like, at least three languages," Jory said. "Well, two for sure."

"I have thumbs," Sasha said. "What?! They don't have thumbs! I could, like, open a jar or something."

"What was the winning talent in the show?" Hunter asked.

Aziz twisted his face up, trying to remember. "Oh! There was a lady bat. And she belted out the famous song from the show."

A collective look of terror swept the faces of the Backstagers.

"Not it," Jory said quickly.

"Dude, if I sing, we'll be bat food," Beckett said.

"Well, someone has to sing!" Aziz said.

"But who?" Reo asked.

And then, suddenly, a beautiful voice filled the chamber singing a mournful melody.

REMEMBRANCE

I REMEMBER THE OLD DAYS

I WOULD SCREECH IN THE MOONLIGHT

STRETCH MY WINGS TO THE SKY
IF YOU LISTEN
MY SONAR GUIDES YOU BACK TO YOUR DEN
AND REMEMBRANCES LIVE AGAIN.

All of the bats perched on the edges of the chamber squealed in delight and Old Chiroptera shut his eyes in great pleasure.

"Oh crap," Beckett said.

A single bat rose up from the depth of the cavern, carrying Bailey Brentwood in its talons. She held a look of stoic determination as she sang the most famous song from *BATS* with perfect vocal execution.

CATCH ME!
BUT YOU NEVER WILL CAGE ME!
FEED ME FRUITS OF REMEMBRANCE!
I'M A PARTY OF ONE.
IF YOU FEED ME
I'LL TELL YOU MY REMEMBRANCES, TOO
TILL THE MOONRISE HAS BEGUN!

The chamber erupted in shrieks and the exuberant flapping of wings as Bailey's bat lowered her reverently down onto the platform with the Backstagers.

"Bailey," Beckett said as he moved toward her.

"Don't," she said in a tone of voice that stopped Beckett dead in his tracks. She faced Old Chiroptera.

"Ms. Brentwood, never in all of my Black Wing Moons have I been so moved by a performance. It would be my honor to admit you to the Great Beyond."

There was a chime of a bell and elevator doors appeared on the wall of the chamber at the back of the platform.

"Thank you, Your Celestialness," Bailey said. "I would be honored to accept. If I can take my—"

She hesitated for a moment.

"—these Backstagers with me."

"As you wish," Old Chiroptera said.

Bailey bowed and walked toward the elevator. The Backstagers just stood there, stunned.

Bailey turned back and said, "Well, come, if you're coming."

One by one, the others followed her lead. Beckett turned to Aziz and said, "I think I'm in trouble."

"I think we're all in trouble, dude," Aziz replied. "But for now, we're moving on to the next level. Come on."

CHAPTER 18

BAILEY STOOD AMONG THE BACKSTAGERS IN SILENCE AS THE elevator rose up.

Finally, Jory asked, "How did you find us?"

"Adrienne and Chloe took me backstage . . . all the way backstage, at Penitent," she said. "They told me everything. All about the ghost during *Phantasm*, and the artifacts, and where Jory really went during *Lease*, and why Thiasos bought your school. I could have waited around to see if you guys actually made it back in one piece, but I figured you'd just lie to me—again—about where you'd been, so instead I got Timothy and Jamie to drive me to Forest of Arden. From there, I just had to follow the red cord and make my way up the tower."

Beckett shouldered his way around the cramped elevator car to look Bailey right in the eye.

"Bailey," he said. "I am so, so sorry. I never meant to lie to you; this thing is just so big, I didn't know how to tell you. I know you have no reason to trust me again—"

"I'm glad we agree on that," Bailey said. "Because it seems like our whole relationship has been based on a lie, and I really don't know how to move forward from here. Do you?"

"I . . . don't," Beckett said, his throat growing tight. "But I want to. I want to figure it out. I feel like I'm going to fall apart right now."

"Well, save that for later," Bailey said. "For now, we have an artifact to find."

"We're glad you're here, Bailey," Hunter said. "You saved us back there. But one question: If you are so furious with us, why did you come all this way?"

Bailey opened her mouth to speak but, in that moment, realized she had no idea. She exhaled, trying to gather herself.

From the corner of the car, Sasha said, "Because it's our destiny."

They all turned to diminutive Sasha, whose mind was racing.

"What?" Hunter said.

"We needed an Onstager to solve this tower. The tower wanted us to work together. Haven't you realized that? We had to dance in the lobby, act in the forest, and sing in the cave. We got lucky the first two challenges, but when we got stuck in the cave, Bailey showed up, because there was no other way."

"No other way?" Reo said.

"I just have this . . . feeling," Sasha said, "that we're all on this path. I think we've all been on it our entire lives. Why did we all become Backstagers in the first place? Why did Jory move here? Why did Beckett take tap as a kid or Hunter work on *Forest for the Trees* or Aziz see *BATS* or Reo learn to read tarot cards? Why did Rample find the Notebook all those years ago and throw it away, only to have Jory find it again in his first months as a Backstager? It's like the road has been laid for us, long ago, and no matter what we do, our only choice is to walk down it."

The doors dinged open. The Backstagers marveled at the scene outside.

There was a galaxy of stars in a great, open void. Comets shot across the sky and glowing beams of light stretched from star to star in the distance, forming crystalline constellations. A pathway of glass stretched directly from the elevator to a flight of stairs, each glowing a different vibrant color. At the top of the stairs, atop a second glass platform, a stone pedestal displayed a shining, golden book.

"The Show Bible!" Hunter exclaimed. "We've reached the top!"

He crossed the walkway to the stairs and started to ascend them.

"Hunter, wait," Jory called.

Hunter easily dashed up the first few steps, but when he set foot on a glowing purple step, the whole staircase suddenly transformed into a slide, sending Hunter careening back toward the platform.

"Hunter!" Jory cried as he ran to the edge of the walkway and caught Hunter by the hand just as he was about to tumble off the edge of the walkway and fall into the starry abyss below. Hunter looked up at Jory, terrified, as Jory struggled to hold on to him. The others ran up to assist them and, with their combined strength, managed to pull Hunter back to safety on the glass walkway.

Jory wrapped his arms around Hunter.

"That was close," he said. "Too close."

"Now we're even," Hunter said as he squeezed Jory tighter.

They all got back on their feet as the rainbow slide turned back into stairs with a sharp *ka-chunk* sound.

"There's a puzzle here," Reo said.

"Not much to go on," Beckett said, looking around into the nothingness.

"Maybe something in the stars?" Jory suggested.

They all gazed for a moment into the peaceful, twinkling night sky.

"There!" Sasha said, pointing to one glittering constellation in the distance. "Do you see that?"

"Yes!" Hunter said, gazing at the shape. "Oh wow."

"But what does it mean?" Sasha said. "Why is there a constellation of a Gamestation Five and a large cheese pizza?"

"What are you talking about?" Hunter said, confused. "That constellation there? It's a calling desk and a headset. The professional kind, like at Forest of Arden."

"I see a Tony Award," Jory said, straining his eyes. "It says . . . my name. I've won for costume design."

"No, it says mine, for scenic design," Aziz said. "It's . . . beautiful."

"We all see different things," Reo said. "I see a stack of ancient grimoires and a quiet room to be alone in with them."

"What do you see, Bailey?" Sasha asked.

"I see the sign-in sheet for *Sincerely Kevin Sampson* on Broadway. My name is on it."

"What about you, Beckett?" Hunter asked.

"I see . . . Diet Coke. Cases and cases of it," he said, although he was actually gazing upon an image of himself cuddled up with Bailey on a couch in a New York apartment. They were grown-ups, just spending a lazy Sunday together binging TV. It made him incredibly sad.

"What does it mean?" Jory said. "Is it supposed to hypnotize us? Distract us from other clues?"

"This is the clue," Bailey said. "We're seeing our dreams. I know what show this is."

She let her eyes linger on the image of the Broadway sign-in sheet for one more moment before turning back to the rainbow staircase.

"Funny, it's the first show I was ever in, *Josie's Entrancing Technicolor Dreamscape.*"

"Destiny . . ." Sasha said.

"In the show," Bailey explained, "a young girl in ancient times deciphers the dreams of a king. She dreams in vibrant . . . colors!" She rushed over to the foot of the stairs and examined their glowing hues.

"And in Josie's first big number, she lists all of her favorite colors in this catchy tune that I can still sing today. It took me forever to memorize all the colors. It goes, 'She loves red . . .'"

Bailey stepped on the first step, which glowed bright red.

"'. . . and yellow . . .'"

She ascended to the next yellow step.

"'And green, and brown, and scarlet . . .'"

She continued up the next three steps, which were colored just the same as the lyrics of the song, but stopped on the scarlet step and looked to the Backstagers below.

"Here, something's off," she said. "This purple step is the one that sent Hunter back down to the bottom, but in the song, the next color isn't purple, it's black. And look! The next step after the purple one is black!"

She took a deep breath and leaped over the purple step entirely to land on the black step. The Backstagers gasped nervously, but the stairs didn't transform.

"Bailey, that's it!" Hunter cried. "You've got it!"

Bailey continued singing as she climbed, only stepping on stairs which glowed the colors listed in the song.

She finally buttoned the song with, ". . . and BLUE!" as she passed the final blue stair and reached the circular glass platform.

Hunter, Jory, Aziz, Sasha, Reo, and even Beckett cheered from the walkway below.

Bailey approached the gleaming gold tome atop the ancient stone pedestal. She reached out and grabbed it, and it instantly transformed into an unremarkable large, black three-ring binder, filled with modern white paper.

"Don't worry, they always change like that!" Sasha called up. "We don't really know why!"

Show Bible in hand, Bailey walked carefully down the stairs to the walkway, where she rejoined the Backstagers.

One by one, each of them gave her a congratulatory hug and told her what a great job she'd done. Though, when Beckett approached, a hug didn't quite feel right. Instead he just said, "You saved the day. As always."

Bailey gave a polite smile and nod. "Should we do this?"

They all gathered around her as she opened the binder. The front page was totally blank.

As was the next page. And every page after that.

"It's a decoy!" Bailey cried. "This isn't the real Show Bible!"

"No, it . . . has to be," Reo said.

"After all that," Aziz said, stunned.

"Well, if this is a decoy, where is the real Show Bible?!" Hunter asked.

As if typed by an invisible typewriter, one by one, ink letters appeared on the front page and said:

THE SHOW BIBLE IS RIGHT HERE. IN YOUR HANDS.

The Backstagers looked up from the binder, stunned.

"I think I understand," Hunter said. He turned to the next blank page and asked, "What can the Show Bible do?"

As before, words appeared from nowhere.

THE SHOW BIBLE HOLDS ALL OF THE INFORMATION IN THE WORLD. YOU CAN ASK IT ANYTHING.

"Whoa!" Sasha said. "Cool!"

Aziz turned a page.

"How do we defeat Thiasos?!" he asked excitedly.

THE SHOW BIBLE CAN ONLY TELL YOU THINGS THAT ARE ALREADY TRUE. IT CANNOT PREDICT THE FUTURE.

"Hmm," Aziz said, disappointed.

There was a moment of quiet consideration.

Then, Jory turned a page and asked, "What happens when all of the legendary artifacts of the theater are gathered?"

WHEN ALL SEVEN LEGENDARY ARTIFACTS OF THE THEATER ARE GATHERED, THE COLLECTOR CAN SUMMON THE CREATOR OF THE THEATER, THE BACKSTAGE, AND ALL OF THEIR POWERS: DIONYSUS.

Everyone stared at the page.

"Dionysus . . ." Beckett said. "The Greek god of theater."

"But that's just a myth," Aziz said.

"Seems like it's not," Reo said.

Jory flipped a page and asked, "Why does Thiasos want to summon Dionysus?"

THE SHOW BIBLE CAN ONLY TELL YOU THINGS THAT ARE ALREADY TRUE. IT CANNOT READ THE MINDS OF—

Jory flipped the page again and asked, "What can Dionysus do when summoned?"

DIONYSUS CAN DO ANYTHING.

"Well, I don't like the sound of that," Bailey said.

"When I was captured," Jory said, "Aleka was talking all about Thiasos wanting to make theater 'pure.' They think that it has come too far from what it was in the beginning."

"So they want to summon Dionysus to . . . what?" Hunter asked. "Wipe everything clean? Start over?"

"I'm not really sure what that would mean," Jory said. "But that's what I'm thinking."

"Well, at least we have this one artifact," Beckett said. "Even if they manage to get to the tower, they'll never find an Onstager like Bailey to reach the top of it, right? I mean, who knows more about theater than Bailey?"

Ding.

Everyone's faces fell as the elevator doors behind them whooshed open again.

They turned and saw, to their horror, the double-faced soldier step out of the doors, flanked by Madam Thiasos, her security guards, and the five young Thiasos Backstagers, Aleka, Niko, Dia, Dimitri, and Tasia.

"We meet again," Madam Thiasos said.

CHAPTER 19

"MOM? DAD?"

Kevin McQueen knocked tentatively on the door frame of the opulent living room where his dad and mom sat silently, their noses in a book and a newspaper, respectively.

"Yes, dear?" Mrs. McQueen said, not looking up.

"Can I talk to you about something?"

"Sure, son," Mr. McQueen said, also hypnotized by his reading.

Kevin stood waiting for a moment before he said, "I mean, like, now."

The elder McQueens lowered their reading and looked sleepily at their son.

"Yes?" his father said.

"Well, I wanted to talk to you about Blake. We . . . we haven't been getting along so well lately."

"Honey, that's terrible," his mother said through a yawn.

"Yeah," Kevin continued. "So we're actually running for Drama Club president separately this year. I wasn't sure if you knew that."

"No, we had no idea," his father said, examining the contents of his glass before he drained the rest of the drink.

"Yeah . . . so, that billboard you bought for him. That was just for his campaign and not mine, so I was wondering if you might—"

"What billboard, honey?" his mother asked.

". . . The big campaign billboard over Maple Avenue."

His parents stared blankly.

"The one you paid for."

Mr. McQueen looked to Mrs. McQueen and said, "We haven't bought any billboard, son. I would never have authorized that."

"Things are a little . . . tight . . . with the economy right now," Mrs. McQueen added.

"But don't worry! We'll be fine! . . . I think."

"Where is Blake, anyway?" Mrs. McQueen asked. "I haven't seen him all day."

Mr. McQueen shrugged and went back to his novel.

Kevin furrowed his brow, totally confused.

"But if you didn't pay for it, who did?"

CHAPTER 20

AS THE DOUBLE-FACED SOLDIER APPROACHED SLOWLY, THE Backstagers huddled around Bailey and the Show Bible, though they all knew it was futile. They were outnumbered and totally cornered.

"We have dozens more soldiers waiting downstairs," Madam Thiasos said. "There is certainly no escape. Hand over the Show Bible. Quickly now, come on."

The double-faced soldier extended his gloved hand.

"We can do this the easy way or the hard way," Madam Thiasos said.

Bailey scanned the room as she clutched the Show Bible tight against her chest.

The Thiasos team at the elevator doors.

The staircase behind her.

To each side, the void of the dreamscape.

They really were cornered. But what was her goal, really? To keep the Show Bible, or to simply keep it away from Thiasos? Maybe she wasn't totally out of options.

"Sorry, guys," Bailey said and, with a grunt of effort, she chucked the Show Bible as hard as she could off the edge of the walkway. It flew, pages fluttering into the darkness.

"Aleka!" cried Madam Thiasos as her daughter swiftly pulled out the Designer's Notebook and slashed her pencil across its pages.

A vast net appeared instantly below the walkway, catching the Show Bible.

Bailey gasped, but the Backstagers just sighed in defeat. They had seen the power of the Designer's Notebook before, and they knew it was just one of the legendary artifacts Thiasos possessed. Very soon, they would have them all.

The double-faced soldier reached into his Carpenter's Belt and pulled out a generous length of rope, which it tossed to the two security guards. One lowered the rope down to where the Show Bible rested in the net while the other began to climb down to retrieve it.

"It was a good idea, Bailey," Beckett whispered. "But they have the other artifacts. We never stood a chance."

Madam Thiasos chuckled.

"The hard way, then. Aleka?"

Aleka began to scribble again.

Beckett met Bailey's eyes, looking miserable, before suddenly, ropes bound his arms and legs, and he fell to the floor.

One by one, Bailey watched her friends become ensnared until finally, she felt ropes twist around her like growing vines until she couldn't stand anymore. The Backstagers lay in a heap, defeated.

"It's gonna be okay. We're all okay," Hunter whispered over and over again.

The security guards returned from the void with the Show Bible in hand and reverently presented it to Madam Thiasos.

When she took the binder in her hands, she shuddered as if overwhelmed by it.

"We've . . . done it," she breathed. "Thiasos has gathered the legendary artifacts, at long last! Soon, we will bring about the Final Blackout!"

"Final Blackout?" said Hunter.

"And you needed us to do it," Jory said. "Don't forget that."

Madam Thiasos narrowed her eyes and hissed, "Throw them in the Prop Box, please."

The double-faced soldier unclipped the box from his belt and walked over to where the Backstagers lay bound. He set the box on the floor, opened it, and began to pick up Sasha.

ANDY MIENTUS

"No!" Aziz cried. "Why imprison us? You got what you wanted! It's over! We lost! Now let us go!"

"I will, I promise," Madam Thiasos said. "After the ritual is complete. You lot have given us enough trouble. We can't risk you interfering with our work until it is done. Then you'll be released, safe and sound. But for now . . ."

She gestured to the Backstagers and the double-faced soldier tossed Sasha into the depths of the Prop Box. The security guards and Thiasos Backstagers joined the soldier, and one by one, they sent each of their prisoners into the darkness of the Prop Box.

When the last of them had been disposed of, the double-faced soldier bent to lower the lid of the box.

"Wait," Madam Thiasos said, her heels clicking on the glass walkway as she strode to where the soldier stood.

"You've done well," she said, "but your most important task is still ahead of you."

The double-faced soldier cocked his head to the side in confusion.

Then with a grunt, Madam Thiasos pushed the soldier hard in the chest, sending him tumbling backward into the open Prop Box.

As he fell into the blackness, he screamed with the voice of a very frightened and confused male teenager.

CHAPTER 21

"EVERYONE OKAY?" HUNTER WHISPERED IN THE DARK.

"Yeah," Beckett said. "I mean, you know. But yeah."

"Does anybody have a light?" Reo asked.

"I do," Aziz said, "but I can't reach."

"I dropped a lantern down here," said a familiar voice.

The Backstagers stopped their struggling. It was very quiet for a moment.

"Who is that?" Jory asked.

"Hang on," said the voice. "Let me find the lantern and then I'll untie you."

There was some fumbling in the darkness and then an electric lantern flicked on, illuminating the space.

They were in a simple wooden room, just large enough

to hold the lot of them. Standing in the corner, holding the lantern, stood the double-faced soldier.

The Backstagers cowered in fear from the masked figure.

"What?" he asked. "Oh, right! The mask."

He reached up and removed his two-faced mask.

"Blake?!" Bailey said.

"Hey, guys," Blake McQueen said. "I'm really sorry about all this."

"You'd better leave me tied up," Beckett said. "Because I'm afraid if you untie me, there might be trouble."

"Let me explain," Blake said. "While I untie you all. Just please let me tell you everything before you jump to conclusions."

"Like the conclusion that you betrayed us?" Aziz said.

"Let him talk," Hunter said.

Blake put down the lantern and set about untying each Backstager. "Thiasos contacted me just before *Tammy* tech and told me everything. At first, they only wanted information from me about where you might be keeping the artifacts. But Kevin was getting stranger and stranger and they warned me that soon, he'd be permanently under the spell."

"Spell?" Reo asked as his ropes came loose.

"I tailed you during tech for *Tammy*. That's how I found the Greenroom and the Arch Theater. The night of the Dance at the Gym, you were all so distracted on the dance floor, I was able to bring them in through Genesius's own stage door and lead them to the Arch Theater. They'd already been in town for weeks. That's how they found out Genesius was in trouble financially and decided to buy the school."

Sasha's ropes were next, then Aziz's.

"Anyway, in the Arch Theater, we encountered the ghost girl, who complicated things. I thought we could get the artifacts out without having to involve you. You guys have been through enough."

"But why?" Hunter asked as he stood and stretched. "Why would you help them?"

Blake looked at him seriously. "Because you've all been in incredible danger. The longer you were exposed to the artifacts, the stronger their effect on you became. And on my brother."

"Effect?" Jory said.

"The way the artifacts hypnotized you all," Blake said. "It was clear to me that Kevin wasn't himself anymore. I was losing him. I didn't understand why we were growing apart. But then, thankfully, Thiasos reached out to me. Backstagers, please understand that the Thiasos are the rightful ancestral owners of the artifacts. They know how to handle them and they were only trying to help you all by obtaining them first."

He freed Jory, who said, "No, that's . . . that's a lie."

"We weren't hypnotized at all," Aziz said. "We were trying to gather the artifacts to keep them safe."

"Safe from what exactly? What are you afraid of Thiasos doing with them? You don't even know what their motive is, but you've all put yourselves in grave danger trying to get them first. You've become obsessed. That's their spell."

He untied Bailey and helped her to her feet.

"Honestly, don't you want to just give it up and let things go back to normal? Thiasos told me that when all this is over, everything at the school will get better and you'll be free to run the theater again. You won't be able to go into the deep backstage, obviously, but you'll be able to crew like normal kids at a normal theater. No ghosts, no monsters, no treasure hunts for magical items, just shows. That doesn't sound so bad, does it? Don't you ever just want to be ordinary teenagers?"

Hunter looked to the floor. The thought had been on his mind more than ever lately.

"I mean, do you guys really think you know more about the backstage and its artifacts after a couple of years than these people do after studying it for centuries?"

He freed Beckett last, who kept his cool as best he could.

"What I do know is you're down here with us," Beckett said. "So it's looking like maybe you've been tricked."

"Yeah," Blake said. "I . . . don't know what to make of that. Where do you think they're taking us?"

For what felt like an eternity but might have only been a few minutes in the backstage, the prisoners of the Prop Box sat in silence, too scared or angry or confused to say anything.

It was a terrifying shock, then, when the ceiling above them suddenly pulled away to reveal a giant Aleka peering down over them. The silence of the last few minutes was broken by terrified screams.

"Blake," Aleka's voice boomed, "come with me. It's time."

She reached a massive hand into the box and scooped Blake up like a toy doll as the other kids scattered to the four walls.

First Blake felt like he was being lifted, then he felt like he was falling, and then he felt his feet beneath him on the ground. He opened his eyes to find that Aleka was no longer giant-sized at all. She stood next to him, equally proportioned, holding the Prop Box.

They were standing in a twinkling void. Blake knew they were in the tunnels of the backstage, but that could mean they were anywhere.

He looked inside the Prop Box and saw tiny Backstagers shouting up to him, but he couldn't make out what their squeaky little voices were saying. He turned to Aleka, furious.

"Just *what* was that little move?" he asked. "The terms of my employment were very clear, and I certainly never agreed to being chucked into a box with a bunch of angry Backstagers."

"Oh Blake, you agreed to help us see our goal through to the end," Aleka said. "We couldn't have you taking off before the most exciting part."

Two Thiasos security guards in sharp black suits rounded

a starry corner at the end of the tunnel. The shorter, female guard pulled out a gleaming pair of handcuffs, and Blake knew that whatever was about to happen, there was no escaping it.

He didn't struggle when they handcuffed him and led him through the tunnels to a stone archway. As they stepped through the arch and exited the backstage, the real world materialized around them.

They were on a ledge of a rocky cliff that overlooked a churning, dark sea. Rows and rows of stone benches faced where they stood, and every seat on every bench was filled with a figure, their identities concealed by the dark robes and howling stone masks. Torches burned around the perimeter of the space, and somewhere off to the side, two masked figures pounded rhythmically with their hands on ancient drums. Looking down, Blake saw that the dirt floor he stood on was adorned with strange symbols, small plates of bread and fruit, goblets of wine, and bowls of swirling incense. He realized that this space was some kind of large altar and he was standing at its very center.

Ever since his earliest memories as a little boy, Blake McQueen loved being the center of attention. However, with rows and rows of lifeless, black stone eyes staring at him, he felt less like a main attraction and more like a main course.

CHAPTER 22

DO THESE HAVE TO BE SO ILL-FITTING?" DIMITRI ASKED, PULLING AT his black ceremonial robes in a hopeless attempt to make them flattering.

"Dude, our families have been waiting for this day for thousands of years and you're worried about fashion?" Dia asked.

"I'm not an animal," Dimitri replied.

"I like them!" Tasia squealed as she spun around and admired the way the robes caught the air. "I feel like the grim reaper!"

They were in their dormitory once again, but now, thankfully, the doors were unlocked, and they could come and go as they pleased.

"So . . . has anyone thought about what happens next?" Niko asked tentatively as he examined his stone mask.

"We summon Dionysus and bring about the Final Blackout, of course," Dia said. "We've only meditated on it, like, every day since we were kids."

"Well sure, but what does that actually mean?" Niko said. "Has anyone actually thought about what happens *after* the Final Blackout?"

"What do you mean?" Dia asked.

"I mean, if we remove all the electricity from the earth, how will people travel? Will everyone only have access to information in books we can get our actual hands on?"

"You can't seriously be second-guessing this now," Dimitri said, rolling his eyes. "You could have said something years ago. You could have, I don't know, *not* put yourself and all of us at such risk to find the Designer's Notebook."

"Well, I never had much of a *choice,* did I?! We were born into this! And then there's Aleka. She's always been the good Thiasos girl, so devoted to the cause. If I'd rebelled, I would have lost her for sure."

He sat on the edge of his bed, his mind reeling.

"I guess I just never thought it would happen in our lifetime. It seemed like make-believe. But now here it is. I've just realized how little we actually know about this thing we've devoted our whole lives to . . . how little she *told us.*"

Tassia took another twirl and said, "I'm sure the elders have a plan—"

"But how will banks work? Or cash machines? Will people have their whole life savings wiped out and have to trade their possessions just to eat? And what about the people with medical problems who need the electricity to survive?"

"What are you saying, Niko?" Dimitri asked.

"I'm saying, haven't you all considered that people could die?!"

Tasia squealed in delight. Dimitri rolled his eyes and turned his attention back to the robes. Dia, however, lowered her head and said, "Huh."

"It's been on my mind," Niko confessed. "That, and now, something else. Why did my mom need to chuck the McQueen kid in the box with the others? His job was done."

"Not done yet," Aleka said from the door. She closed it behind her and made for her corner of the room where her robes lay waiting.

"There you are," Niko said.

"'Not done yet'?" Dia asked. "The kid helped us find the Genesius artifacts and then solved the tower for us so we could get the Show Bible. What else could he possibly do?"

"We're summoning Dionysus," Aleka said. "He's going to manifest in a physical body for the first time in eons."

Dia made a gesture as if to say, *And?*

Aleka smiled.

"Where do you think that body is going to come from?"

The other Thiasos kids stood shocked for a moment. Finally, Tasia understood the implication.

"OH! You mean, like, a sacrifice?!"

"Sorry to disappoint you, Tasia, but no. The McQueen boy will live, but he'll share his body with our great patron. Naturally, his life won't really be his own anymore. He'll be a passenger in the vessel of his body, rather than the pilot. What an honor to host the great architect of the backstage as Thiasos brings forth a new era of global rebirth with the Final Blackout."

She clipped a pin to hold her dark robes together and admired them in the mirror, her eyes alight with anticipation.

"Well, that's not nearly as cool, but okay." Tasia pouted.

"I just hope this doesn't take too long," Dimitri said. "This fabric is really irritating my sensitive skin."

Dia glanced silently to Niko, who returned her look of concern. They both knew it without having to say it. Maybe they did have a choice after all.

CHAPTER 23

ONE BY ONE, EACH OF THE BACKSTAGERS WAS TAKEN FROM the Prop Box by a suited Thiasos soldier and handcuffed.

"We're in the tunnels," Aziz commented, looking up at the stars.

"What's happening now?" Jory asked. "Where are you taking us? Hello?"

But the soldiers just worked silently until the Prop Box was empty. A tall, thin soldier took the Box and made his way down the tunnel until he rounded a corner and disappeared from sight.

"Form a line," another ordered coldly.

The Backstagers looked at one another tentatively, then did as commanded. Beckett reached for Bailey's hand secretly and she took it. They couldn't talk right now, but they both knew what the other wanted to say just with a squeeze.

"Follow me."

The soldier led them down the tunnel and, after a few twists and turns, through a stone arch and back into the real world. There, a great crowd of masked, robed figures faced some kind of altar where Blake was chained by the wrists to two stakes in the dirt on either side of him.

"Blake!" Hunter cried. Blake looked to Hunter with the terrified eyes of a captured animal.

"Quiet!" the soldier ordered. "Look straight ahead."

"We're at Thiasos headquarters," Jory said. "This is the ancient theater where they captured me!"

"I said, quiet!"

The soldier led the line of Backstagers through the aisle between the rows of masked onlookers to a flight of stairs that snaked its way up the side of the cliff. When the stairs leveled off, they could see a dark, windowless mansion in the distance.

They walked across the lawn to the mansion and the soldier unlocked the front door and barked at them to go in.

The lobby of Thiasos headquarters was a darkly gorgeous hexagonal room with purple velvet curtains, inky paintings of Thiasos members past, iron candelabras that twinkled with candlelight, and a grand wooden staircase leading up to the next floor.

The soldier took them across the lobby to a heavy wooden door to one side of the grand staircase. He pulled it open, revealing a shockingly modern steel staircase spiraling downward.

"This way."

The Backstagers plodded down several floors, to the very bottom of the stairwell. Beneath flickering halogen lights, there was a white hallway lined with black doors with small barred windows.

"Awesome," Beckett said.

"This way," the soldier commanded.

Using one of the keys from the ring on his belt, he opened a door and gestured for the Backstagers to enter, which they did, begrudgingly. It was a simple cell with a couple of metal benches and, thankfully, a door to a small bathroom.

"Oh, thank goodness," Sasha said before darting into the bathroom.

The others dropped onto the benches.

"Did you guys see Blake?" Hunter asked.

"Yeah, that looked pretty murder-y," Aziz said. "What do we do?"

"I don't know what we can do," Hunter said.

"They wouldn't hurt him, would they?" Bailey asked.

"They didn't hurt me when I was captured," Jory said. "But this is all getting crazier and crazier."

"I'm just glad we're all here, together," Beckett said. "I mean, I'm sorry you've gotten dragged into this, Bailey. This was the last thing I ever wanted to happen. That's why I kept it from you. But, just my luck, here you are, in danger anyway. Still, I have to say, I'm glad you're here."

"I think I get it now, Beck. I think I'd have a hard time telling someone I'm close to about this if I were in your shoes. But still, just know honesty is the best policy with me when we get out of this."

"Ha, if."

"*When.*"

There was a toilet flush and Sasha emerged from the bathroom looking relieved in more ways than one.

"You're looking awfully optimistic," Reo said.

"Why not?" Sasha said. "I still believe what I said back in the tower. I feel it more strongly than ever. We're exactly where we're supposed to be."

Suddenly there was the sound of a key in the door. The Backstagers all rose and gathered in the middle of the room, ready to face whatever was coming next, together.

The door swung open to reveal Niko and Dia.

"Ugh, you two," Jory moaned.

Niko tossed something to Hunter, who caught it, even though his hands were cuffed. It was a key.

"Do your cuffs with that and help Dia and me do the others," Niko said. "We don't have much time."

"Whatever game this is, can we just skip it?" Jory said.

But Hunter's cuffs came free, and he looked to Jory, surprised.

"The artifacts are all assembled on the altar, so it won't be long now," Dia said. "The trick, though, is that all of the artifacts are out of the backstage. Meaning they have no special power. It's a window we can use."

"Why are you helping us?" Aziz asked as Hunter undid

his cuffs. "You were part of the crew that trapped us here in the first place."

"This has gone further than we planned," Niko said. "We knew we were summoning Dionysus. They never told us he'd need a human body as his host."

"I don't like the sound of that," Reo said.

"Your friend is in danger," Dia said.

"'Friend' is a strong word," Aziz replied before Hunter shot him a reproachful look.

"There will be a hundred or more devotees down at the theater, but they are unarmed," Niko said. "And, as Dia mentioned, the artifacts have all been laid out on the altar and they have no power in the mundane world. It will be tricky, but if we can surprise the horde of soldiers and get to the artifacts, we might have just enough time to throw them into the sea and destroy them. There's no telling what Thiasos will do to us after that, but at least the Final Blackout will have been averted, and your friend will be safe."

"The Final Blackout?" Hunter asked.

"It's Thiasos's ultimate goal," Dia said. "To command the power of Dionysus to wipe out all the electricity on the planet and bring the world back to the old ways. It's a mission we were born to achieve. We just never thought we'd live to see the day when it might actually happen. But now that it's here, we've finally figured out that it's not a future we want to see."

"All of the electricity on the earth . . ." Bailey whispered. "That's—that's terrifying!"

"We have to stop them," said Hunter.

"Jory, you spent the most time with these guys," Beckett said. "It's your call. Do we trust them?"

Jory took a hard look at Niko and Dia. Niko had deceived him for weeks during *Tammy*, but he had shown him kindness after the truth had come out in the ancient theater. And he distinctly remembered Dia objecting to taking him hostage after they had taken the Designer's Notebook.

"It's a tough call," Jory said. "But yeah, I trust them. And honestly, at this point, what do we have to lose?"

CHAPTER 24

THE MOON WAS WAXING CLOSE TO FULL ABOVE THE ANCIENT THEATER.
The space had been prepared with chanting and the burning of arcane incenses.

The faithful were gathered, a hundred stone masks staring coldly toward the woman who stood upon the altar.

Everything was in readiness.

"Hail, the Designer's Notebook! Artifact of creation!" Madam Thiasos called out to welcome the sacred artifact. She wore a crown of olive branches and a white ceremonial robe and looked out over the crowd.

"HAIL!"

A robed Thiasos member brought forth the Designer's Notebook with great ceremony and laid it on a stone table a few feet from where Blake knelt, shackled.

"Hail, the Master Switch! Artifact of illumination!" Madam Thiasos cried.

"HAIL!" replied the crowd.

"Hail, the God Mic! Artifact of communication!"

"HAIL!"

"Hail, the Ghost Light! Artifact of protection!"

"HAIL!"

"Hail, the Carpenter's Belt! Artifact of construction!"

"HAIL!"

"Hail, the Prop Box! Artifact of collection!"

"HAIL!"

"And *finally*," she said, with great gusto, "Hail, the Show Bible! Artifact of information!"

"HAIL!" the crowd cheered, and as the seventh artifact was laid on the table with its siblings, the whole gathering on the cliffside went wild with frenzied celebration. The drummers pounded on their instruments with the fury of the thousands of years that Thiasos had waited for this night.

"Where on *earth* are Niko and Dia?!" Aleka whispered to Dimitri and Tasia.

The youngest members of Thiasos sat, robed and masked like all the others, in the last row of the ancient theater.

"This is the most important night of any of our lives, and they're going to miss it!"

Tasia and Dimitri looked to each other, two identical,

clueless stone faces, and shrugged. Aleka looked around nervously.

"IT IS TIME!" Madam Thiasos shouted as a hush fell over the crowd.

The wind that swept across the cliffside grew still. The insects singing in the spring night became quiet. Even the sea itself seemed to soften its crashing to make way for the invocation that was about to occur. Madam Thiasos took a breath, preparing herself, then began.

"Great Dionysus! Creator of the theater and all its magic! Patron of us, your flock, the Thiasos! Rival of Zeus himself! We have gathered your artifacts from the far corners of the backstage and have brought them here, to your ancestral home, to call upon your power. Great architect, we invoke thee!"

A swirl of dark mist began to gather low in the air above the table of legendary artifacts. It was thin and indistinct at first, but it became thicker until it looked like a swirl of storm clouds hanging just a few feet in front of where Blake stood, bound. He stared into the dark vortex, terrified.

Sprinting across the lawn, the Backstagers, Dia, and Niko reached the staircase at the edge of the cliff some fifty feet above the ledge where the ritual was taking place. They saw the swirling dark portal and stopped dead in their tracks.

"We're too late," Niko whispered. "He comes."

"No! It can't be," Hunter said. "Maybe if we get to the artifacts . . ."

"The portal is opening. We've passed the point of no return," Dia said. "Soon he'll arrive and enter the body of the McQueen boy. Because he is chained, they will then be able to command Dionysus to do their bidding and bring the Final Blackout."

Threads of crackling electricity danced around the vortex. The hoard of Thiasos swayed and chanted as if possessed.

"We'd better run," Niko said. "Like, now."

Hunter looked around to his crew and was met with one pair of sad, defeated eyes after another. They'd failed.

Sasha's eyes, however, were fixed in quiet contemplation.

"I know what to do," he said solemnly.

He walked to the edge of the cliff and looked down at the vortex, unafraid.

"My muse came to me in a dream and told me to trust my instinct, when it speaks. And it's speaking now, as loud as anything I've ever heard."

"Sasha, what are you talking about?" Aziz asked.

A tear fell down Sasha's cheek, but he smiled.

"The muse said that I was the chosen one. Don't you see? This wasn't meant for Blake. It's meant for me."

"Sasha, you don't mean—"

But before Aziz could finish, Sasha made a run for it down the stone stairs.

"Sasha, no!" Aziz cried, racing after him as the others looked on in shock.

As he reached the ledge at the bottom of the stairs and sprinted toward the altar, Sasha roared like a warrior charging into battle. The crowd all looked toward the disturbance, a hundred emotionless stone masks glaring at Sasha in unison.

Madam Thiasos's triumphant expression melted to one of horror as she tried to catch the charging little blond boy.

He evaded her grasp, though. The vortex's electricity gathered at the center, and as it built into a blinding bolt of lightning, Sasha leaped in front of the chained Blake McQueen.

"NO!" Aziz cried as he reached for his best friend.

The bolt of lightning surged forth from the center of the dark vortex and hit Sasha directly in the chest with a blast so bright, everyone had to avert their eyes. A deafening crack of thunder erupted around the cliff, louder than a blast of dynamite.

Aziz's ears rang and his vision was blurry as he regained his footing and looked down to the ledge. The vortex had disappeared and Sasha lay on the ground, lifeless. The crowd of Thiasos stumbled to their feet and removed their masks to see what had happened to the boy.

"Oh my gosh," Bailey whispered.

Beckett took her hand. "Is he . . ."

But then his tiny body rose off the ground, into the air, and began to stretch and change.

Aleka turned to Tasia and Dimitri and said under her breath, "We have to run, right now." They nodded, and the three snuck away from the crowd and made their way up the stone stairs.

Light poured from Sasha's eyes. He doubled in size, then tripled, as his round body became chiseled like a classical statue. His blond curls grew spontaneously into a golden mane. With a flash of light, his T-shirt and jeans became a perfect white toga fastened with gold.

Now he was a shining deity straight from the pages of an epic poem of mythology. He was Dionysus himself. He opened his electric blue eyes.

Aleka, Tasia, and Dimitri reached the top of the stairs and were stunned to see Niko and Dia cowering with the Backstagers.

"I should have known," Aleka said to her brother. "Do you know what you've caused? Dionysus is unbound! We cannot control him!"

"I didn't know the boy was going to do *that*!" Niko said.

"What do we do?" Dia asked.

"We take cover in the emergency shelter in the head-quarters," Aleka said. "Come on!"

The Thiasos Backstagers made a run for it across the lawn, but Dia stopped when she noticed that the Genesius Backstagers hadn't budged.

"We're all in danger," Dia shouted. "You have to come with us!"

"Sasha's still in there," Aziz said. "I'm not leaving him behind."

"Good luck, then," Dia said as she ran off with the others toward the Thiasos mansion.

Down on the altar, the crowd groveled on the dirt floor as a disheveled and cautious Madam Thiasos approached the levitating Dionysus as if she were approaching a tiger out of captivity.

"Great deity," she said, trying so hard to project authority into her voice. Dionysus turned and looked pathetically at the tiny human.

"My family has worked for thousands of years to summon you here tonight! We have spent countless hours and many fortunes to procure each of the legendary artifacts. We have brought you back into this world! In return, all we ask is that you take back the lightning that man stole from the gods. Strip the earth of all electricity and technology. Take us back to the old ways. Make theater, and the world, pure once more! And we, as your flock, will worship you in a new, better world!"

Dionysus cocked his head to the side and said, **"My flock?"** with a voice that sounded like a thousand voices. **"You don't seem much like a flock to me. A flock doesn't command the shepherd. A flock doesn't attempt to chain the shepherd to the ground."** He gestured to the limp Blake McQueen, who had fainted in his terror, still bound by each wrist.

Madam Thiasos swallowed hard. She knew she'd made a terrible mistake.

"But more than anything, where are your horns? A flock ought to have horns," Dionysus said with a smile.

"Wh-what?"

"Let me help," Dionysus said, and with a sweep of his hand, Madam Thiasos sprouted horns, then hooves, then fur, and in moments had transformed completely into a black goat. She opened her mouth to scream, but instead, a piercing bleat rang out over the cliffside.

One of the Thiasos members looked up and wailed at the sight of what their leader had become. A stampede began, as the entire crowd panicked and tried desperately to escape the ledge by climbing up the single narrow staircase that led to safety.

Dionysus waved his hand again and now, more than a hundred goats of various colorings scrambled up the cliff-side. They passed the hiding Backstagers in a herd and galloped off through the lawn of Thiasos headquarters toward the woods beyond the mansion.

Dionysus laughed a thunderous laugh.

The Backstagers cowered behind the rocks at the top of the cliff.

Aziz stood from his hiding spot and began to descend the staircase.

CHAPTER 25

WHAT'S THIS? ANOTHER DARES APPROACH ME?"
Dionysus roared at Aziz, who, though tall for
his age, looked minuscule as he descended the
stairs toward the towering deity.

"I . . . I actually want to speak to the other person in
that body you stole," Aziz said.

Dionysus snorted in disbelief.

"Say that again, boy."

"I said I'm not talking to you, I'm talking to my best
friend, Sasha. Sasha, buddy, I know you're still in there.
And I need you to fight and take your body back!"

Up on the cliff, the others watched in disbelief.

"What is he *doing*?!" Hunter hissed. "He's going to get
himself turned into livestock. Or worse!"

"Just listen to my voice and come back to me," Aziz said. "I'm not leaving here without you, buddy!"

Dionysus rolled his eyes and said, **"Enough of this,"** as he raised his hand. Aziz cowered and braced himself for whatever his fate would be.

But then Dionysus's hand went limp, and his fingers curled strangely, as if he were suddenly paralyzed. He looked to the hand, stunned, and tried to move it, but it hung there as if it were held in place by an invisible shackle.

"Oh my gosh," Jory said from his perch. "It's working."

Aziz looked at Dionysus's hand, amazed, and continued.

"I can't imagine school without you, Sasha. Heck, I can't imagine life without you. You know I love all the Backstagers, but we go back to even before our time as Backstagers. Every good memory I have, I share with you. All those opening nights, all those Gamestation marathons. That time I got the runs during *Les Terribles* tech and you covered for me."

Dionysus laughed, but it was Sasha's voice.

"I can't imagine making more memories without you. I won't do it!"

"I won't do it, either," Jory said. He'd descended the stairs and now stood shoulder to shoulder with Aziz. "I know I've only been with the Backstagers for a year, but already I love you like a brother."

"We all love you, Sash," Beckett said, joining them. "Plus, I really don't wanna have to train another kid to take over the light board, so do me a solid, please, and come back to us."

Dionysus began to sway as if feeling faint. The rest of the Backstagers raced down the stairs.

"Come on, Sasha, you beat that weird rash-dragon you got that one time, and you can beat this!" Hunter said.

"I sense great power in you," Reo said. "Banish this spirit back to his own realm."

"Your crew needs you, Sasha!" Bailey said. "And I need you, too. You're a really good friend."

Dionysus now drifted back to the earth and shut his eyes as if he were fighting a migraine. Aziz stepped forward and touched Dionysus's massive leg.

"So either you kick this jerk back to Olympus or we all become goats or whatever, but we're not leaving without you. Backstagers stick together!"

Dionysus fell to one knee, panting. Sasha's voice emerged from his lips.

"Guys . . . Thank . . . you . . . I love you all . . . but . . . I'm . . ."

His eyes snapped open, wide like a frightened animal, glowing brilliant blue.

". . . I'm losing."

Suddenly Dionysus stood again as the sound of thunder ripped across the cliff and a shock wave sent all of the Backstagers flying backward toward the steep drop and raging black water below.

"I'm impressed," Dionysus said. **"Your friend is strong and your bond with him is special. But tell me why I shouldn't cast you all off into the sea right now for challenging me?"**

Aziz stood and brushed himself off.

"Thiasos stole our artifacts so they could summon you

into a chained body and command you to do their bidding," he said. "We don't want anything from you. We don't even want your artifacts. We just want our friend back. Surely you don't need his body."

"Maybe I like having a human body," Dionysus said. **"It's so boring in the realm of the gods. It's been ages since I've had any fun."**

"And picking off tiny, weak humans is fun?" Aziz asked.

Dionysus looked to the other Backstagers, who had gathered themselves up off the dirt and now stood united with Aziz.

"Your friend is good," he told them. He thought for a moment and then said, **"You're right, I want a challenge. In the backstage, where the real fun is. Each of you, take an artifact and meet me there when you're ready. If you can impress me with a show of your strength, I will leave your friend's body unharmed and return to my realm."**

Aziz looked to his left and to his right as each of his friends nodded bravely.

"We accept," Aziz said.

"Then I shall meet you in the backstage. For the final confrontation."

"But where?" Aziz asked.

"Where else?" Dionysus said. **"In the Arch**

Theater. Choose your artifact and ready your-selves, Backstagers. This is the final act."

With that, Dionysus turned into pure golden electricity and shot like a thunderbolt into the cave in the cliffside, through the stone arch portal, into the backstage, leaving the others there alone.

Aziz exhaled. He learned from his brief stint as an Onstager that he could act a little, but pretending to be brave in the face of an angry demigod should have earned him a Tony.

"Am I dead?" Blake McQueen moaned from the altar, stirring back to consciousness.

"No! Thanks to Sasha, none of us are," Bailey said as she hurried over to help him up.

"Where is Sasha?" Blake asked groggily.

"We'll explain in a minute. First, let's get you out of those chains. Hmm, maybe . . ."

She scanned the ground for the pile of robes that had until very recently belonged to a human Madam Thiasos and searched them for the key. She found it and freed Blake, who rubbed at his sore wrists.

"What are we going to do?" Aziz asked. "It's good we bought ourselves more time, but even with the artifacts, I don't know how we're supposed to defeat a demigod in battle."

"But he didn't say we had to defeat him in a battle," Bailey said. Everyone looked at her quizzically. "He said we had to impress him."

She walked over to the table of artifacts. They looked so ordinary outside of the backstage, with no special power. A notebook, a binder, a microphone, and so on. But just like theater itself, these humble materials are so much more than what meets the eye when imbued with the magic of the backstage.

She picked up the Show Bible and walked into the cave, toward the stone arch.

"Bailey, where are you going?" Beckett asked.

"I need to ask the Show Bible something."

She stepped through the arch and was now standing in the twinkling darkness of the tunnels. She opened the Show Bible to a fresh page.

"What impresses Dionysus?"

CHAPTER 26

THE BACKSTAGERS MARCHED THROUGH THE TUNNELS TOWARD their final challenge in the Arch Theater, united and unafraid.

Beckett lit their path with the Master Switch while Reo cast a circle of protection around the group with the Ghost Light. Aziz was armed with the Carpenter's Belt while Jory wielded the Designer's Notebook, just in case they ran into any obstacle on their journey that they needed to tear down or build a bridge across. Bailey and Blake pored over the Show Bible, asking it question after question about the backstage and how it all worked. Hunter carried the Prop Box and God Mic, which weren't of much use now but soon would be vitally important. Still, he wanted to feel useful, as stage managers often do, so he used the God Mic to blare some music from an epic film soundtrack, gearing them all up to end this thing, once and for all.

"We need to make a pit stop in the Tool Room," Aziz said. "There's something I wanna get before we head into the theater. Kind of a secret weapon."

✂

After taking care of Aziz's errand, they set course for the Arch Theater.

Before long, a vast red-velvet curtain emerged from the formless darkness of the tunnels, and they knew they were there.

"This is it, guys," Hunter said. "Before we go in there, I just want to say what a pleasure it is to call you my crew, all of you. Not even a demigod can take that away from us."

He looked to each of them.

Aziz, so driven and passionate. Always focused on the solution, not the problem.

Beckett, as intelligent and skilled as he was adorably caffeinated.

Reo, already such an integral part of the team. What did they ever do without him?

Bailey and Blake, two Onstagers who actually gave actors a good name. Maybe. Most of the time. He couldn't believe how bravely they'd faced this strange new world when it meant saving their friends.

And Jory, his person, the guy who he found endlessly

fascinating and inspiring. Not to mention cute. Like, puppy-in-a-hoodie kinda cute.

"We ready?" Hunter asked.

"Born ready," Beckett said.

"Let's bring our boy home," Aziz said.

"So mote it be," Reo said with a nod.

"About time you asked me that," Bailey said.

"If we *must*," Blake said with a wink.

"Then let's do this," Hunter said, as he drew back the red curtain and they all stepped through, into the Arch Theater, the very heart of all theater magic.

Dionysus sat like a king on the edge of the mezzanine. He was so large that he took up the entire level as if it were one seat, his legs dangling off the balcony rail, nearly touching the orchestra level below.

"Welcome, Backstagers of Genesius."

"Well, you look comfortable," Aziz said.

Dionysus narrowed his glowing blue eyes.

"Shall I rise? Are you ready to show your strength?" He flexed a giant muscular, golden arm.

"No, you sit back and relax," Bailey said. "The show is about to begin."

Hunter took up the God Mic and spoke into it, *"PLACES! BACKSTAGERS, THIS IS YOUR PLACES CALL! EVERYONE AT PLACES, PLEASE!"*

THE BACKSTAGERS AND THE FINAL BLACKOUT

The Backstagers nodded and scattered into the wings.

Jory took a pencil from behind his ear, opened the Designer's Notebook and began to sketch. As he drew, a lush velvet curtain swept across the lip of the stage.

Beckett slid the Master Switch downward as the lights in the Arch Theater dimmed dramatically.

Jory drew a piano in the Notebook and a real piano just like it instantly appeared in the pit.

Blake McQueen stepped out into the light, took a bow, and descended into the pit, Show Bible in hand. He sat at the piano, set the Show Bible on its music stand, whispered something to it, and opened it to reveal a full musical score. He began to play.

It was the dramatic introduction of "By Myself," the plaintive anthem of unrequited love from *Les Terribles*.

The curtain swept open, revealing the iconic Rainbow Barricade set from the show.

Aziz pulled flare after flare out of the Carpenter's Belt, launching them over the stage like pyrotechnic cannon fire.

"Hm," Dionysus said, raising a golden eyebrow.

From his spot in the wings, Reo tossed the Prop Box onto the stage.

Its lid popped open and from it, Bailey Brentwood emerged, costumed just like the doomed heroine she'd played in Genesius's production.

Beckett slid the Master Switch again and the stage was

bathed in a gorgeous theatrical light cue. A spotlight hit Bailey just as Blake reached her entrance in the music.

She tore into the song and somehow sounded even better than she had in its original run. Her acting teacher always talked about how higher stakes made for better acting, and what could make the stakes higher than performing for the mythical creator of theater itself?

BY MYSELF

BUT IT'S JUST LIKE HE'S WITH ME

IN MY MIND

I STILL CAN FEEL HIM KISS ME . . .

Beckett watched her from the wing, full of pride and affection. The last time he'd heard her sing this, they were best friends. Now that they'd shared a kiss in real life, the lyrics hit his ear in a new way. He hoped she'd still want to kiss him again if they all got out of this in one piece.

Bailey reached a crescendo in the song as Blake transitioned the music to a new tune, more rhythmic and contemporary.

"HERE COMES THE TRANSITION," Hunter whispered into the God Mic. "SCENIC AND LIGHTS . . . GO!"

The entire Rainbow Barricade set disappeared with a few slashes of Jory's eraser and Bailey leaped back into the Prop Box, disappearing from sight.

Beckett made an adjustment to the Master Switch and

now the lighting was colorful and pulsating, like a rock concert. A new set appeared line by line: a city street scene with fire escapes and run-down brick buildings covered in graffiti.

Bailey emerged from the Prop Box in a new outfit, looking like a 1990s grunge girl ready to go out on the town.

Aziz reached into the Carpenter's Belt and drew out a leaf blower. He turned it on high and a breeze blew from the wings through Bailey's flowing dark hair like she was in the greatest music video ever.

She was now in the fully realized world of *Lease*, the tragic rock opera. She began to sing.

THERE'S NO RE-DO
NO SECOND TAKE
MAKE THIS DAY COUNT
YOUR LIFE IS WHAT'S AT STAKE
LET'S HIT THE ROAD
DON'T BE AFRAID
TODAY'S OUR ONLY DAY . . .

Blake modulated to a new, spookier tune as Aziz presented a fog machine, spraying a thick, low-lying mist all across the stage.

"*LIGHTS!*" Hunter called into the God Mic as Beckett flicked the Switch again and everything went dim.

Jory erased the *Lease* set and quickly sketched some flickering candelabras.

Bailey reached into the Prop Box and pulled out a simple white robe, which she slipped over her grunge clothes, transforming instantly.

Reo entered from the wing, his black sweater and hat obscuring his face, clutching the Ghost Light like a wizard's staff. It cast a ghostly light over the fog.

Bailey and Reo paced around each other in a circle as she sang, as if hypnotized,

HE'S HERE

THAT FABULOUS PHANTASM!

I FEAR

THAT CURIOUS PHANTASM!

AHHHHH!

Bailey sang the challenging vocal section of Crystalline's big solo from *Phantasm* with the skill and passion of the greatest Broadway soprano. As she nailed the infamous high note, the set once again was swept away to a blank slate as the lights faded and the music transitioned.

The tune was a rock anthem, written to be performed for stadium-sized crowds. This time, when the lights faded back up into a colorful wash, the set was bare scaffolding with the back wall of the Arch Theater still visible. Bailey emerged from the wing in a simple T-shirt and jeans. She closed the medley with the epic finale from *Tammy.*

WHEN I'M WITH YOU, I FEEL THE MUSIC
WHEN YOU'RE WITH ME, WE HEAR THE
BEAT
WHEN I KISS YOU, I TASTE CRESCENDOS
I SENSE THE RHYTHM IN YOUR FEET . . .

Blake played the keys like a rock star on his farewell tour.

Hunter called cues with the precision of an air traffic controller.

Aziz pulled duel confetti cannons out of the Carpenter's Belt and fired blast after blast of glitter around the space.

Beckett slid the Master Switch up and down, creating a dazzling spectacle of color and light.

As Bailey held out the powerful final note, Reo pulled their secret weapon out of the Prop Box: a small purple tool mouse whose turquoise tongue lashed about as it bounded out from the wings and scurried up onto Bailey's shoulder.

"Friendo?" Dionysus whispered in Sasha's voice.

Lights flashed, confetti rained down, Blake ran his hands up and down the keys like a madman, and Bailey belted like a rock star, until finally Hunter called, *"BLACKOUT!"*

Everything went quiet and dark.

When the lights faded back up to simple work light, the whole St. Genesius crew stood in a line across the stage. Friendo still clung to Bailey's shoulder affectionately.

She stepped forward.

"That's our strength," Bailey said. "The magic we create when we work together."

Dionysus sat expressionless for a moment.

Everything was silent.

Then, he started banging his hands together wildly. Each time they collided, lighting flashed and a deafening boom echoed through the theater. It was truly thunderous applause.

"BRAVO!" Dionysus cried. **"That was spectacular! The best show I've seen since the opening night of** *Medea*, **twenty four hundred years ago!"**

"So you were . . . impressed?" Hunter asked.

"Most supremely," Dionysus said with a golden grin. **"I had a feeling all those years ago that you'd be the crew to use the artifacts for the good of the theater. I was right to have led you to this day."**

"Led us? You had this planned all along?" Beckett asked, amazed.

Dionysus just grinned mischievously.

"Anyway, a deal's a deal. I will relinquish your friend's body as promised. But first, I have one more deal to offer you."

"What is it?" Jory asked.

"Protect my artifacts as your own and use the magic I created in the backstage to spread

beautiful theater all your lives," he said. **"In return, I will bless and protect each production you ever work on from my seat in the realm of the gods."**

Each of the kids nodded. The theater had chosen them just as much as they had chosen the theater. There was no other answer.

"Farewell, Backstagers," Dionysus said. **"And happy trails."**

He clapped his massive hands once again, and with a blinding flash, he vanished completely. In his place, Sasha lay in the aisle of the orchestra.

"Sasha!" Aziz cried as he raced down the aisle to his best friend.

"Is he okay?!" Hunter asked.

Aziz cradled Sasha as he groggily opened his eyes.

"Did . . . did anyone get a pic of me when I was in god mode?" he said.

Everyone burst out laughing and cheering.

"He's fine!" Aziz said as he hugged Sasha tightly.

Friendo leaped off of Bailey's shoulder and scampered up the aisle into Sasha's arms, licking the giggling boy with his turquoise tongue.

"You did good, crew," Hunter said as he embraced the others in a bear hug. "Now let's go home!"

EPILOGUE

HOUSE LIGHTS TO HALF," HUNTER CALLED INTO THE HEADSET.

"Copy," Sasha said, sliding a control on the light board.

"Everyone at places?"

"Jory here!"

"Reo here."

"This is Aziz."

"Beckett here, obvi." Beckett smiled at Hunter from his spot just next to the calling desk.

"Alright Sasha, bring 'em up."

Sasha brought the stage lights to full, revealing a bright and cheery cue splashed across Aziz's set of a simple podium and a festive sign that read, CONGRATULATIONS, GRADUATES! all across the back wall.

There was a hearty cheer from the packed house as Ms. LuPone entered and took her place at the podium.

"Welcome!" she said. "Friends, family members, faculty, and, of course, our new graduating class!"

There was another enthusiastic roar from the audience. It took Ms. LuPone several attempts to quiet them down so that she could continue.

"It is my distinct pleasure to be able to lead this ceremony today. As you all well know, St. Genesius hasn't had an easy time of it these last months. We almost had to sell the school to a private company. But miraculously, they had a change of heart and decided to fund our school from afar and leave the Genesius founders in control of the school. Therefore, let's give our special thanks to the Thiasos Organization for their generous support."

As the audience applauded, Beckett said into the headset, "Yeah, thanks, Aleka. It was the least you could do."

"Go easy on her," Jory said. "Niko and Dia said she's really struggling with all those goats to care for."

Everyone cracked up, and they were all very happy to be stifling laughs over the headset again like old times.

"Now, without further ado, may I give you our graduating class!"

One by one, Ms. LuPone announced each of the seniors and they entered from the stage right wing, crossed to the podium where Ms. LuPone gave them their diploma, and exited stage left to cheers.

For Timothy and Jamie, however, their crosses were a bit different. Timothy entered to flashing colored lights and a sudden jolt of music blasting over the sound system, a pop diva wailing her dance hit. Jamie got pops of streamers from cannons Aziz had installed in hidden chambers in the sign. The guys all cheered over the headset for each successful prank as Ms. LuPone rolled her eyes and smiled. Backstagers will be Backstagers.

When each graduate exited stage left, they were ushered by Aziz through a door to a hallway, which they followed back into the auditorium. However, when Timothy and Jamie got their diplomas, they were instead met by Jory, who said, "Come with me," ominously.

As Quentin Quackenbush began to give his valedictorian address, Jory arrived in the Club Room with Jamie in tow. Timothy was waiting there on the ratty sofa, still in his cap and gown.

"Okay, we're both here," Timothy said. "*Now* can you tell me what's going on?!"

Jory just put his finger over his lips and walked over to the Unsafe door. He opened it wordlessly and gestured for them to enter.

"Fair enough," Jamie said, chuckling.

Timothy and Jamie stepped through the Unsafe door into the tunnels, where they found a mysterious red thread tied to the inside doorknob. It stretched invitingly into the abyss.

"After you," Jory said.

The three of them followed the thread through twists and turns until they reached its end at another doorknob. The door was rough around the edges, as if it had been hastily sketched into the blackness of the tunnels.

"Shall we?" Jamie asked.

"I think we'd better," Timothy said.

They opened the door and stepped inside. Jamie gasped. Timothy took Jamie's hand.

They were all there.

Hunter and Aziz and Beckett and Sasha and Reo and Bailey and even Friendo stood on the stage of the Arch Theater, which had been decorated with beautiful hanging lanterns and draped streamers, but that wasn't all. Blake and Kevin McQueen, reunited as brothers and as copresidents of the drama club, gave identical waves. The Backstager girls from Penitent Angels were there, too: Vivian in her signature black hat, Amber looking stylish as ever in hoop earrings, tall Genevieve smiling uncharacteristically, Juniper, whose ginger pompadour rivaled Hunter's in height and structural perfection, and, of course, Adrienne and

Chloe, who held each other like sisters as they wiped fresh tears from their eyes. Mr. Rample and Bert stood off to the side, where they'd just put the finishing touches on a lavish pizza party spread. Spectral Phoebe hovered above them all holding the Ghost Light, ever their protector.

Everyone began to applaud. Timothy and Jamie began to cry.

"Ha-HA!" Bert cheered.

The boys from Genesius raced forward and scooped the graduates up in a group hug as the others continued to cheer. Time was always fluid in the backstage, but it was the friendship contained in that group hug and not the magical theater where it took place that made the moment seem to last forever.

When the hug finally broke, Hunter tapped a few symbols on the God Mic, filling the theater with thumping music as the party began. Sasha and Aziz practically pounced on the snack table while Hunter gave Jory a spin, starting a dance party toward the lip of the stage. Reo caught eyes with the enigmatic Vivian and tipped his black hat in greeting. She tipped hers back, and the two came together by the punch bowl to meet. Beckett was off in the wings fiddling with the Master Switch to get the perfect disco-ball cue when Bailey approached.

"You guys pulled off the surprise," she said. "Congrats."

"Yeah," Beckett said, suddenly nervous again around the person he'd always felt closest to. "I can't believe none of the guys ruined it."

"Well, you're all pretty good at keeping secrets," Bailey said with a smirk.

Beckett turned a bright pink and began to stammer when Bailey let him off the hook.

"I'm messing with you," she said.

Beckett laughed and dropped his head guiltily. "I wish I knew how to make things right again," he said.

"I'd start with the truth. The whole truth. I bet you guys have some pretty amazing stories from the backstage."

"Oh, totally," Beckett said. "A million of 'em. It's been a wild ride."

"Well, how about you tell me the best ones over pizza this weekend? You're buying."

"You mean like a date?" Beckett asked.

"Well, are you gonna make me spell it out for you?" Bailey asked with a laugh. Beckett couldn't help but smile and was relieved to see Bailey smile right back, just like old times. They stood like that for a wonderful moment before the music lowered and Mr. Rample stepped to the middle of the space, raising a plastic cup of punch to make a toast. Everyone gathered around.

"Timothy, Jamie, congratulations on a legendary run as

Backstagers here at St. Genesius. You have led a team like no other I've seen and raised them up to be worthy successors. I know the next generation will make you as proud as you've made me."

Timothy and Jamie smiled at Hunter and Beckett, who nodded with the confidence required of the next official stage managers of St. Genesius.

"In fact, you have done such impressive work," Mr. Rample continued, "that Bert and I would like to offer you both positions on the professional crew at the Forest of Arden Theater. Jamie could begin immediately, and Timothy when he completes his studies at Wolverine University. I hope you'll both accept."

Jamie opened his mouth to speak but could only sob tears of joy as he embraced Mr. Rample.

"Can I take that as a yes?!" Rample chuckled.

"Yes. Yes, of course, it's a yes! How can I ever repay you?" Jamie said, wiping his tears.

"Oh, kiddo, this is me repaying you! You passed the magic of theater on to the next generation, as they will someday do themselves. It's like the great song from *A Casting Call* says: 'the gift is ours to borrow.'"

Everyone gathered around: a circle of outsiders who became friends, all for the love of theater and the tradition and lore that came with it.

Rample looked to each of them and said, "We've all seen a lot of fantastical, mysterious, impossible things in our time in the backstage, but the most magical thing of all about being a Backstager is the community. For all the ups, there will be many downs in your lives as artists. That's the price you'll pay for doing what you love. But your community is what will keep you going through all of it, just as it has in your time here at Genesius. Backstagers are kindred for life, across generations. As long as outcasts come together in the dark to make magic, we'll all be together."

Jory's breath caught in his chest as he thought, for the first time, about what it would mean to be a Backstager for life. His first year with his crew had been filled with unimaginable dangers, terrifying monsters, and grueling

challenges. It had also been the best year ever. Looking around at his fellow outcasts, he couldn't imagine a better way to spend a life or a better crew to spend it with.

THE END

ACKNOWLEDGMENTS

Once again, I must express profound gratitude to Maggie Lehrman for leading me to the Backstagers and guiding me so expertly through this process and to Rian Sygh and James Tynion IV for trusting me with their world and characters. It's been one of the great honors of my career to take your story forward.

Big applause to Emily Daluga and everyone at BOOM! for their invaluable input, Andrew Smith and everyone at Abrams/Amulet for welcoming me to the best home a writer could ask for, Hallie Patterson for helping me get the word out and joining me on adventures to the Bronx, and Geoff Soffer for nailing it behind the scenes, whatever I do.

ANDY MIENTUS is an actor, singer, and songwriter who is best known for his roles in *Spring Awakening*, *Wicked*, *Les Misérables*, *Smash*, and *The Flash*. He lives in New York City.

RIAN SYGH is a comic artist and cocreator of the award-winning Backstagers comics. He lives in Glendale, California.

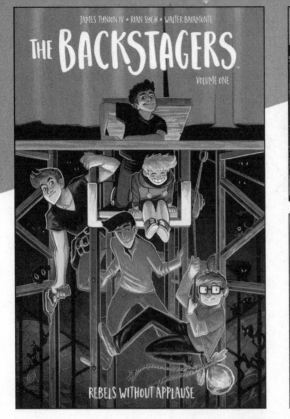

IT'S TIME FOR AN ENCORE!
SEE WHERE THE ADVENTURE BEGAN IN

THE BACKSTAGERS™

THE GRAPHIC NOVELS THAT INSPIRED THE NOVEL! AVAILABLE WHEREVER BOOKS ARE SOLD

f /BOOMStudiosComics 🐦 /boomstudios 📷 /boom_studios boomstudios. t